Backs Against the Wall
Survival Series
Book Two
By Tracey Ward

<u>Dedication</u>

*For my husband Lawren who taught me about zombie
cage fighting, trebuchets and Greek Fire.
So much badass would be missing from this book were
it not for him.*

Tracey Ward

Chapter One

I may be a Tinkerbell, but I'm definitely Tink when she's trapped in the lamp gasping for her last breath, begging the world to believe and clap their friggin' hands. In essence, I cannot fly. I know it the second my foot leaves the ledge. I feel it when I go airborne. I've done this sort of jump enough to know my limits, to know when I'll get hurt and when I'll be fine, and I absolutely know it now.

It's too far.

I tuck and roll the best I can, but gravity is unkind. I've gathered momentum, too much to be useful, just enough to be hurtful, and I tumble head over shoulders over side over elbows onto knees. I'm pretty sure I did a cartwheel back there somewhere, something I wish my mom could have seen. She spent hours with me in the backyard one sunny summer day trying to teach me how to do them. I always managed to land on my head. She eventually called it, telling me to give it a rest before I hurt something important. It's advice I wish I'd remembered back up on that higher roof. Now as the skin of my face is left somewhere 10 feet back, my right cheek having taken a hell of a blow on the rough tar rooftop, I also remember something else important.

I never liked Tinkerbell. She was a jealous jerk who deserved what she got and worse.

Finally I tumble to a stop on my back, smacking my head hard against the ground until I see stars.

"Ow," I mumble weakly.

I'm not sure what I'm complaining about. There's too much pain to inventory all at once. I'll have to take stock of my body one limb, muscle and burning abrasion at a time. This will take a while. But the good news is I have nothing but time. The zombies are still out there, very nearby I might add, and I have no clear idea of how I'm getting off this roof now that I worked so hard to get here. If I go inside this building, I'm going in blind and defenseless. I don't know what the situation is in there, if there even is one. Way my luck is going, there is. No doubt about it.

I move my legs. First the right, then the left. No breaks, good news. There's a pulled muscle or two down there but nothing I can't handle. My arms are next. Right one, good. Left one—

"Holy Mary Mother of God Almighty," I grind out through gritted teeth as I roll back and forth on the ground trying to escape the pain. "Oh yeah, that's broken. Soooo broken."

My language goes far downhill from there. Jack and Jill tumbling down and breaking every bone along the way kind of downhill. I take a few deep breaths, vowing to never move my left arm again, and I test out the rest of me. Neck is good. That's a relief. Head is sore along with the face but I haven't begun vomiting, no dizziness, no blurred vision. Odds are I took a hard hit but no concussion. Ignoring the left arm (something I dare you to do someday. Go ahead, break it and pretend it never happened. Can't be done!) I'm alright. I'm mobile. I've got a snowball's chance in hell of surviving this. But I know I can't do it alone. Not with a broken arm and limited defenses.

I reach for my trowel, ready to take another shot at signaling for help despite my I-Am-Wonder-Woman-And-Need-No-Man moment back there. Independence is great but real strength is being able to ask for help when you need it. And man oh man, do I need it right now. I won't sit around wishing and hoping someone will save me, but I do understand I have to keep trying to get help. I'm going to expose myself to the biggest, baddest gang out there if all goes according to this terrible, suicidal plan, so announcing myself to any other gang out there is really no big deal. Unless it's the cannibals. Screw those guys. I'd rather be zombie dinner than end up on their plate. At least the zombies can't feel feelings any more, making them sort of blameless. What's the cannibal's excuse? Crazy, that's what.

Unfortunately, my trowel is no longer with me. I sit up, hugging my arm to my chest, and give out a groan but otherwise the pain is being handled internally. I broke it somewhere near the elbow because all I can feel is white hot pain in that area. I refuse to look at it though. I know I'll see bone and I can't handle that now. It's too real. If I see how truly awful, crazy, jacked up bad it is, I'll give up. I'll imagine it hurts worse than it already does and I'll assume I'm dead meat. I need denial to make it out of this alive.

I scan the rooftop for the trowel but it's MIA.

"Perfect."

Alright, no more calls for help. I wanted to do it alone and it looks like that's what I'll do. I stand up slowly, letting my skin stretch in new ways that tells me where more cuts and scrapes are. To be clear, by 'scrapes' I mean road burn. I mean sections of skin lost to the rooftop like it was trying to make a Joss suit it could wear. My thin Colony clothes are ripped wide open in several places making them nearly useless. I'm shivering again, something that's working wonders for my arm, so I get moving to warm up. Also to seek shelter. I don't know that I'm going home, though.

The way I see it I have two options. I'm in no condition to see The Hive today. They prey upon weakness and in my current state I am all weak sauce, so I can go to Crenshaw to have him bandage me up or go to Ryan. That's it with that second option. No real benefits, no promise of help or healing. Just Ryan. One choice is smart, one is emotional and I hate, loathe and despise emotional. But can you imagine which option I'm considering the hardest?

I make my way to the door leading off this roof. I'm relieved when it opens easily. I was worried it would be locked as so many these days are, like my water sources all are. Not that it seems to matter since people still break into them and rob you blind. My temper flares, fueling my aching body with the steam it needs to get down the long flight of stairs, through the seemingly endless corridors and out into the growing morning light.

There are Risen everywhere.

They haven't spotted me yet. In fact, most are heading toward the building I jumped from, probably answering the siren call of the other Risen still pounding on a door to the rooftop to get to me. But in my current state, openly broken and bleeding all over the road, it won't take long for them to catch my scent. As it is, I'm bleeding steadily from my arm onto the pavement.

I turn quickly, taking off at a fast pace as I pull the hem of my shirt up high until my left arm is cradled in it against my chest. I ball up the excess fabric in my right fist as much as I can to pin my injured arm in place. I feel tears sting my eyes as what feels like sandpaper against raw nerve screams from my elbow through my entire body. I have to bite my lip to keep from crying out. To keep from basically waving to the Risen and saying, 'Hey! Over here! Breakfast is served!'

With my shoddy makeshift sling in painful place, I run. I book it as fast as my sore, sorrowful legs will carry me. I dart down alleys trying to avoid Risen but they're everywhere. I can't get away from them and I find eventually that my best bet is to run right down the center of the street dodging them when I have to. Hands reach for me, mouths snap toward me, but it's nothing I'm not used. I tune it out and focus up. But all the focus in the world can't make me fast enough to outrun this city.

A Risen tackles me as I try to dart out of the way. She grabs onto different parts of my body as she slides down the side of me while I try to continue to run. I'm using denial again, pretending I absolutely do not have a 130 lbs zombie hanging from my waist right now. Eventually she slips down far enough that I think I'll escape but she grabs my leg and we both hit the pavement hard. Luckily I'm able to roll onto my back. It's good news for my busted arm, my face and my life. Never, never, never ever let a Risen get your back. You can't fight them off, you can't hold them off. If they get ahold of you from behind in any way, especially pinning you to the ground, we'll all miss you and say lovely words at your funeral because you're dead.

She grabs onto the waist of my pants, trying to use

it to climb up me but the best she gets is pulling the loose material down my hips slightly. I roll as far as I can away from her then I swing back toward her where she rests on my leg, bringing my free knee up and putting all of my force and momentum behind it. I'm able to crack her right in the face, stunning her enough to scurry back, clearing my feet from her grasp. I'm in no condition to fight her any more than this so I roll over on my good arm and use it to help hoist me up onto my feet. My nearly useless sling is now completely useless so I cradle my left arm with my right, noticing some interesting textures there and doing everything I can to not think about what I'm touching. Then I run.

I run until my lungs burn. I run until my legs are rubber. I run until the Risen have thinned and I have a chance to stop for two seconds to try to catch my breath so I can run some more. The only good thing about today so far is that it's just that; day. I can see. I have landmarks to tell me where I'm heading and whether or not I'm running in blind circles surrounded by a sea of Risen. I'm still really far from home. Maybe too far. I might have to take up residence in one of these buildings soon, definitely before nightfall.

I know I need to get moving but I can't. I can feel it in my entire bitter body. I haven't slept, I haven't eaten and I'm fading fast. I need water soon for sure and a bandage or fifty would be nice too.

"You don't want to stop here," a voice calls quietly from down a dark alley nearby.

I jump to attention, nearly leaping out of my ruined skin.

"This is The Eleven's territory," he continues. "They'll eat you alive."

He's nothing but a motionless shadow wrapped in

darkness. A vague form inked in black on black paper.

"Are you one of them?" I demand, sounding fiercer than I feel.

"No."

"Then you shouldn't be here either. Why don't we both leave and no one has to get hurt?"

"I thought you wanted me to come."

I scowl, thoroughly confused. "What?"

"Your signal."

The trowel. The light.

"You saw it?"

A figure steps out slowly, emerging from the shadows by degrees. Tall, blond hair. Kind of gangly. But it's his eyes that I notice more than anything. They're razor sharp, slicing my momentary strong façade to shreds. He sees it. He sees how broken I am. Because he sees everything.

Trent.

"Didn't you want me to see it?" he asks softly.

I hesitate, unsure. I did want him to see it. But now that he's here I'm not so sure. His eyes are too intent on my face. His demeanor is too calm considering our situation. He's knee deep in another gang's territory, there are Risen everywhere around us and yet he stands there casual as can be as though the world never went all out Daffy Duck a decade ago. I could sense it when I saw him in the woods, but now standing in front of him with his eerie eyes on me, I'm burning with it. This guy is completely and utterly unnerving in every way.

My hesitation has drawn out to over a minute, I'm sure of it, yet he says nothing. His stance, his gaze; none of it changes as he waits for me to respond. We've gone well beyond the norm of social convention, even in the apocalypse, and I'm starting to feel twitchy. These days, time is living and we're wasting a whole lot of it staring at each other like idiots out here in the open.

"I did," I say too quietly. I straighten my aching back and try again. "I did want you to see it. I thought…"

"You thought what?"

God, his tone is even. Like a machine. The way my father's alarm clock used to sound. *It. Is. Now. 6. 30. In. The. Morn. Ing. Rise. And. Shine.*

"I thought you might help me."

"Why would I do that?"

I narrow my eyes at him. "Why are you here?"

His mouth twitches ever so slightly. "What do you need?"

Isn't that the question? I need a bed to sleep in. I need water to drink. I need food to eat. I need help with my beaten body. I need Crenshaw is what I need.

"I need you to take me to Ryan," I say firmly.

If he's surprised, he doesn't show it. He doesn't show much of anything.

"What do you need with Ryan?"

"Good, so you admit you know him."

"What would be the point in denying it?"

"Does that mean I can stop pretending I don't know your name, Trent?"

"Apparently it does."

This time he allows a grin. It changes his face entirely. He goes from the intense, horrifying robot boy that was giving me chills to a young man with a nice smile. The instant transformation is creepier than anything else about him so far. It's too sudden, too extreme. Like watching a mask come off only to find the person underneath is not who you expected at all.

"You know who I am too, don't you?" I ask, taking

a gamble.

The grin disappears. Robo Boy is back. "I don't know your name."

"It's Joss."

He nods in understanding. That's it. No other response.

"You've seen me before, haven't you?"

"I've seen everyone before."

"I believe it," I say wholeheartedly. "You saw them take me."

"Yes."

"And you've seen me with Ryan."

"Several times."

"Does he know what happened to me?"

"Yes."

"Because you told him?"

He shakes his head. "Because he's smart."

"Does he know you're here now?"

"No."

"Why not?"

"Did you want me to bring him?"

I pause, not because I don't know the answer but because I don't know if I want him to know it. But then again, I'm pretty sure this guy knows everything already.

"Yeah," I admit quietly, "I did."

"I didn't want him to see you dead."

My heart leaps into my throat, my skin covered instantly in pins and needles as adrenaline courses through me. I take a step back from him, scanning him quickly to check his weapons. Like it matters. If he has even one, he outmatches me. Hell, just having two arms is a victory for him. But knowing I'm the underdog won't stop me from fighting. Never has, never will.

"Relax," he says, the grin reappearing. I wish he'd put it away. "I'm not going to hurt you. I didn't want Ryan to come with me in case I got to you too late. If you were dead, he didn't need to see that. I'd rather he thought you were alive in the Colonies than dead in the streets."

It's the most he's spoken by far, making it possible to notice how hypnotic his voice is. It's deep and melodic, the evenness not so creepy after all. Maybe even kind of nice. I don't relax, though, and I don't give back the step that I took. I've seen enough predators to know that the ones that draw you in are the most dangerous. Case and point – Vin.

I look around us at the unfamiliar buildings that could be swarming with Risen or Eleven, neither of which I could survive an encounter with.

"So you'll help me?"

"I'll try."

I nod my head as I take that crucial step toward him, muttering, "That's all any of us can do."

The first thing Trent does is makes a sling for my arm. He has a backpack strapped to him full of various supplies, most of which I only get a glimpse of, but I do see weapons. Plenty of them. Hammer, wrench, ginormous knife. My fingers are itching to get their hands on one of them so I'll feel a little more like myself and a lot less like a damsel in distress, but when you're out in the wild with nothing to your name but a thin set of clothes, bruises and a broken arm, there comes a point where you have to admit defeat.

"This is a mess," Trent tells me plainly as he winds a long sleeved shirt into a makeshift sling, his gaze leveled on my arm.

"It sure feels like it," I grumble, trying to ignore the

fact that gazing at my arm pulled in tight to my body also means gazing at my breasts. I'm hoping Robo Boy is too preoccupied with the gnarly nasty that is my arm to worry about my assets.

"Have you looked at it?"

"No."

"Smart."

"It can't be that bad."

"It's bad."

I don't know why I do it. Probably because I feel like I'm being challenged. Like he thinks I can't handle it or something. The wild is a competitive place and proving you're strong is proving you can survive. I'm already standing here helpless as a toddler with my pride piddling down my leg onto the street. It's shameful and I hate it.

So I look. You know, to prove I'm hard.

I immediately turn my head and vomit.

"Told you not to look," Trent chides.

He takes this opportunity to slip the shirt around my injured arm, spiking the pain I'm already feeling from unbearable to black-out-off-the-charts. I'd vomit again if I had anything left. He steps behind me, something I abhor, and ties the sleeves of the shirt firmly around my neck.

"There," he says gently. "It'll feel a little better soon."

I run the back of my sleeve over my mouth, removing the clinging bile.

"Thanks," I mutter.

"We need to move. People are coming," he says abruptly. I feel his hand on the small of my back urging me forward. Like his words a moment ago, it's surprisingly gentle.

"How do you know that?" I whisper.

"I can hear them. They're on the fire escapes," he whispers back.

I can't hear anything, but I trust that Trent absolutely does so I move beside him as quickly as I can.

"In here," he whispers as he ushers me into a doorway. It's deeply recessed, a lot like mine at home, and it reminds me of the night I watched Ryan from it. The night I made the decision that changed everything.

"Won't they see—"

His hand clamps over my mouth as he pushes me farther into the shadows in front of him, his back to the street. It's then I notice he's dressed almost entirely in dark gray and black. He uses his free hand to pull the hood of his sweatshirt up over his blond hair and suddenly he's completely indistinct. He's way taller than I am, but still I cower down so my head is hidden behind his body. Seeing that I understand, he releases my mouth.

It's not long before I hear the fearless trample of footsteps. It's the kind of walk only the gangs can have. The security in there terrain, their numbers, their unashamed existence. The Lost Boys can all afford to be loud. It's almost like a badge they wear stating they're unafraid. Why should they be?

Trent and I listen to them cruise down the street. I hear at least three different voices but there are more than that. These three are just the loudest.

"How much longer until the next market?" one calls out. "I need my fix."

"You'll go broke dealing with that mess."

"Shut up!"

"Eight days, dumbass," someone else says. "Learn

to count."

"I'll learn to count when you learn to read, genius."

"I can read just fine."

"Yeah, right! You can't even spell your own name."

"Maybe not but I do know sign language. What does this say?"

I hear laughter disappearing down the street, then the faint cry of, "Screw you too!"

Trent doesn't move a single muscle. He stays perfectly still, his face hovering over me with unfixed eyes. He's listening, probably hearing things I can't make out anymore. I don't dare speak a word because I know how to survive. You have to be patient, you have to be smart and most of all, you have to be quiet.

"We're clear," he finally says, his deep voice reverberating in the confined space.

When he steps away, I instantly feel cold. I hadn't realized how freezing I was until the pain in my arm began to fade a little. Now that I have a chance to focus on it and I got a taste of what warm could be huddled next to Trent's body heat, I'm very aware of it.

"You don't have an extra coat in there, do you?" I ask reluctantly, gesturing toward his backpack.

He frowns. "No. I can give you mine."

"No," I tell him quickly. "No thanks. You need it for the camo, shadow thing you do. I'll be fine."

"We'll move faster. It'll warm you up."

I nod as I fall into quick step beside him. He doesn't speak at all. I'm not sure if it's because he's busy listening or because he doesn't like to make with the small talk. Either way, I like it. I've lived alone a long time and I don't especially care for chit chat either. It's a little intense, this complete silence from him, but the longer we walk together the more I feel myself relax. We're not exactly best friends yet, but considering he hasn't killed, molested or sold me, I think we've got a shot at not being mortal enemies. I'm counting that as a win.

Chapter Two

It's a mile but it feels like a hundred. It takes less than an hour but it feels like years. By the time Trent slows us down to circle around his gang's building, I'm panting and sweating from pain, exhaustion, exertion – you name it. If he would stand guard over me while I lay down on the sidewalk and took a nap, I'd do it in a heartbeat. But something about his no-nonsense attitude toward everything makes me think that isn't happening.

We encountered a few Risen along the way. I got to sit uselessly idle, tucked safely away against a building with my back to the wall, watching as he worked his magic. Trent is quick and efficient. He doesn't strike a blow that doesn't serve a purpose. Every use of his energy is a gain for him, every assault is dealt with a higher purpose. I'm good, don't misunderstand me, but sometimes I get frantic and start whacking away at things, beating them to a pulp until they can't come at me anymore. It's exhausting and as I watch Trent, I realize it's wasteful. And emotional. That dirty word that won't leave me alone. Or maybe it's been with me longer than I think, I'm only just noticing it now.

"We're going to go in a side entrance," Trent tells me, his eyes fixed on mine. I am powerless to ignore him and that stare. "Don't make a sound. Don't ask any questions. Don't leave my side. Do you understand?"

"Yes."

"Good."

"Wait."

His jaw clenches for a split second. "What?"

"Where are you taking me?"

"Inside the den," he says slowly.

"No, I get that. I'm asking where you're taking me once we're inside. You're obviously hiding me, but I want to know where."

"Ryan's room."

"Does Ryan have a roommate I should worry about?"

"Yes and no."

"You wanna take a second and spell that out for me?" I ask, feeling annoyed.

"Yes, Ryan has a roommate. No, you don't have to worry about him."

"Why not?"

"Because it's me."

I take a deep, calming breath. "Wouldn't it have taken less time to simply tell me that instead of making me play 20 Questions with you?"

"It would have taken less time to not answer you at all. We could inside by now. Anything else you want to ask?"

"So many things, but they can wait. For forever probably. Let's go."

He leads me across a small side street into an alley. It's filled with debris both from buildings and life in general. I see soiled mattresses, ripped clothing, fractured plastic pallets, a large satellite dish that I'm guessing came from the roof and just piles on piles of who knows what. Trent jumps on top of a large section of the garbage, a section that I believe to be a true industrial sized garbage bin, but it's so buried and rusted I can't be sure. He makes the leap then lands silently, like a cat. A tall, creepy, cryptic cat. His eyes scan the alley, then the roof, then the wall of the neighboring building, me, some garbage and then a window with a sill sitting at nearly eye level for him. He's processing all of this on some next level that I'll never understand, mapping it out in his mind and cataloguing it for future use. Or for fun. Maybe attention to detail is how he gets his jollies.

He makes an abrupt motion with his hand, calling me toward him. I have to bite my lip against a cry of agony when he helps me up onto the garbage pile. My left arm is jostled around roughly, and while I tried so hard to leave it slack and never to use it, I still instinctively flex it several times. Liquid lava pumps in my veins as Trent peers through the window. He eventually pries it open, then gestures for me again. He hoists me up onto the sill like I weigh nothing at all and carefully pushes me inside. There's a table on the other side that I slip down onto, no problem.

I look around, taking in my surroundings. The first thing I notice is the smell. Living in the apocalypse you learn to deal with rancid smells. Rotted everything is everywhere, the most popular of which is rotted wood and textiles. Carpets, couches, rugs, clothes. They get so full of mildew that almost all of the buildings smell of it. But not here. Here the first thing I smell is burning. It's a clean, campfire kind of smell. Strong, dry wood snap crackling with warm orange flames. It's probably what's heating this place. A furnace or fireplace lit somewhere feeding in warm, dry air that chases the moisture away. It's a luxury I've never had living alone.

My fires are always dire circumstances, life or death types. Always secret, always scary. And while the Colonists had power and warmth, it wasn't like this. It was sterile and electric. This is sort of... homey. It reminds me Crenshaw.

I kind of hate it.

Trent leaps silently into the space beside me, his eyes immediately roaming the empty hall we've entered. After several beats, he takes my uninjured hand and begins to pull me forward. I jerk my hand away, my heart racing. My skin burning.

He looks back, his face concerned.

I shake my head dismissively, feeling like a psycho, then gesture for him to go ahead.

Bless his cyborg's heart, he lets it go and gets a move on. He doesn't ask why I can't stand to be touched. Why I'm weird. He leads me down a narrow hallway past a series of closed doors. Finally, toward the end of the hall, he opens one and ushers me quickly inside.

The room is small but warm with two beds, one small desk and a window that has been all but boarded shut. The beds are nothing but old, bare mattresses with blankets tossed over them. I notice that the floor is covered in clothes. I glance at Trent in surprise, shocked to see that Mr. Methodical is a pig at heart, but whatever insult or question I had for him dies on my lips. The wall beside one of the beds has been hollowed out, the drywall stripped down, the insulation yanked out. In its place is shelf after shelf secured between the wood. On those shelves are more books than I can ever remember seeing in one place. I'm sure I went to the library at some point as a child, but I honestly can't remember and right now, I really do not care. Even if those libraries of the old days had housed a million books, they couldn't compare to this. To one wall full of treasures saved and preserved in a world where everything and everyone wastes away to ash and dust.

"They're Ryan's," Trent tells me, seeing my stare. "He's a bit of a collector."

"Little bit," I mutter in agreement.

"That's his bed on that side if you want to lie down and rest. He won't be back for another few hours. You may as well get some sleep."

I feel myself blush at the idea of laying in his bed. Honestly, I think I'd be more comfortable laying in Trent's. There's something less... I don't know. Meaningful about it, I guess. Sleeping in Ryan's bed? I almost feel like I'd enjoy it too much.

"I don't want to bleed on his bed," I say lamely, gesturing to my jacked up arm.

Trent quirks an eyebrow at me, not buying it. "You're giving his bed more credit for cleanliness than it deserves."

"That doesn't really entice me to jump right in."

Trent shrugs before taking a seat on his own bed. "Stand then. It's your call."

I'm too tired to stand. I'm too beat down, exhausted and aching tired to be proud or embarrassed either. I carefully step through the room, mindful of the piles of clothes on the floor, trying to avoid them and but failing. Then I carelessly collapse on his bed. The sigh that escapes my lips is pure joy leaking from my soul. I slept on a bed in the Colony. It was weird and awesome, but I also resented it. I saw it as a sign of the world being forced on me, of the lie they were all living. But this is different. This mattress is far less comfortable, far more worn and it smells of dude. It has the faint scent of a very familiar soap made by the wizard of the woods and the musky smell of good old fashioned stink. It's earth and sweat. Grass and warm skin.

This I kind of love.

I lay on my right side with my back to Trent (a massive show of trust or a case of too tired to care on my part), my face close to the books in the wall. It's a crazy collection, one I think he built based on availability and not personal preference. I don't recognize any of them. Not until I see the tattered, faded spine tucked in close behind the jagged edge of the crumbling drywall. This one I know immediately.

The BFG.

I want to touch it. I want to pull it out and run through the pages, to get the scent of book in my nose and the feel of the paper beneath my fingers. To read the words and hear my mother's voice in my warm, darkened room at night as I lay bundled up trying not to fall asleep. But I don't because it's dumb. It's a mistake. It's crying waiting to happen and I've shed enough tears in the last twenty-four hours to last me a lifetime. I'm all tapped out on sad today.

So instead, I close my eyes and I fall asleep.

***

"He's coming."

I jerk awake, my arm screaming in pain. I don't know when I fell asleep or how long I was out, but Trent's deep, quiet voice snaps me out of it immediately. I sit up in the bed, pressing my back to the wall so I'm facing the door. Outside it I can hear footsteps and a loud, laughing conversation. It's Ryan. The other voice may be Bray, but I only heard it once before. It's too long ago and too muffled now to tell for sure. Trent sits at the edge of his bed facing the door. Waiting. It takes me only a moment to notice the knife ready in his patient hand.

"What are y—"

"Shhhh," Trent shushes me quietly, his eyes steady on mine and his finger pressed to his lips.

With his creepy, all seeing eyes the gesture is just about the scariest thing I've ever seen.

"I'll get you next time," someone says from down the hall.

"You say that every time," Ryan replies, his voice laughing, "and every time, who wins?"

"I will beat you."

"Every single time."

"Jerk," the other person grumbles.

"See you at dinner."

"Yeah."

The doorknob turns with a creak. I watch Trent's hand clench on the handle of his knife, the knuckles going white. Every other inch of him looks completely calm. I look around for a weapon of my own. Something to attack Trent with before he can get to Ryan. There's nothing. Dirty, holy socks and a worn out muscle tee. Worthless. Who doesn't sleep with a knife by their bed?!

As the door swings open, I hold my breath, my body going rigid on the bed.

Ryan steps into the room. His face is flushed like he was just running. His hair is standing at odd angles, wet around the edges from his sweat. He looks a mess. A vibrant, broad, beautiful mess.

"Hey, Trent, you're back. Where did you go—" Ryan's voice dies out the second he sees me. Then it bursts to life again, far too loud. "What the f--!!! How did--?!?!"

He cuts himself off both times, biting down on his knuckle and dropping into a crouch in front of the door. He isn't looking at me anymore. He's staring at the ground, reining himself in.

Hurried footsteps run back up the hall, heading toward us.

"Ry, you okay?" someone asks. They try the doorknob but Ryan quickly throws the lock. He presses his weight harder on the door. "Open the door, man. What happened?"

"Nothing," Ryan says, his voice tight. "Trent scared the hell out of me, that's all. You don't want to come in. He's naked."

I frown, glancing at Trent. He's grinning.

"Why is he naked?"

"To mess with me. Seriously, it's fine. I'm good."

"Alright," the voice replies. He sounds relieved to be kept on the other side of the door. "Tell Trent to put his gear away."

"Yeah."

Ryan stays crouched down, his back to me, as the footsteps fade. When they're gone, when we all hear the click of a door closing down the hall, he stands up slowly. I watch his shoulders rise and fall quickly with a sharp breath, then he turns to face me. His brown eyes lock on mine.

"How are you here?" he whispers roughly.

I grin, feeling myself glow inside just seeing him again. "It wasn't easy. Your buddy here got me most of the way."

He looks at Trent, his eyes falling on the knife and ignoring it. I relax a notch. "You saved her from the

Colonists?"

"Just the Risen," Trent corrects. He lays the knife on the plastic crate serving as a nightstand beside his bed. It makes me more nervous unattended than it did in his hands. "She did the rest herself."

"And the Eleven," I correct him.

Trent nods slowly in agreement. "But the Colony, that was all you."

"You escaped from the Colonists alone?" Ryan asks incredulously.

I shift in the bed, wincing in pain from my arm. Ryan takes another step closer to me. It's a small room. Two more and he'll be sitting on the bed with me. I hope he has the sense not to do that.

"Did they do that to you?" he asks, gesturing to my arm, his eyes tightening in the corners. "The Colonists, did they hurt you like that?"

I shake my head. "No, I did this to myself while I was running from them. They gave me pie."

"What?"

"Pumpkin. It was really good."

"Then why'd you run?" Trent asks.

I look at him, not sure if he's making a joke or not. His face is stone.

"You are painfully hard to read," I tell him.

"Maybe you're not a strong reader."

"Is that an insult?"

"It is if you take it as one. Perception is—"

Ryan groans loudly. "Trent, come on. It's not a great time for a philosophy lecture."

"Or it's always a good time and you think otherwise due to your perception."

"No, just stop. Joss, we need to do something about that arm. It looks rough."

I nod, fighting the urge to look at it again. If I puke, there's nowhere to do it in this room where I won't saturate something he owns. Something he uses on a regular basis and no matter how many times he washes it he'll remember, always and forever, that *this* was the thing Joss vomited on.

"I don't know what can be done," I tell him. I'm trying not to sound like I'm terrified of the idea of him touching it. Of anyone touching it or moving it, even breathing on it. Why can't we all just pretend it isn't there?

Ryan comes closer, closing that meager gap between us. I'm aware of his smell and his heat, the same smell in the bed only stronger. Closer. Warmer.

He frowns at my arm.

"It needs to be set or it will never heal right. We should splint it too."

"What do you mean by 'set' it?" I ask. I know the answer and I know it'll hurt like crazy, but I have to ask.

He meets my eyes. They look sorry. He's apologizing already for this thing he hasn't even done yet. This things that's going to make me cry again.

I nod my head in understanding.

"Sorry."

"It's okay," I lie. I'm angry at him that he's going to do this to me. It's not his fault, but I'm still angry.

"I'm also sorry we can't do it here."

"Why not?"

"I doubt you'll be able to keep quiet."

I take a deep, shuddering breath, but I don't flinch and I don't look away. "It's going to be like that, huh?"

He grins but it looks more like a grimace. "Yeah, it's gonna be like that."

Chapter Three

Trent has to go to work up in the Crow's Nest overseeing the world, so it's just Ryan and I leaving the building. We go the same way Trent and I came in. Ryan is efficient and agile leaving out the window, like he's done it a hundred times, and I start to wonder if these guys even use the front door to this place.

When we first start walking, Ryan puts his arm around my waist, pulling me in close to him to either support me, guide me or just remind himself I'm really there. Whatever his motives, it makes me nervous and a little scared. I feel trapped. Small and broken beside his strength. When I gently shake off his hold, he doesn't say a word. In fact, we both stay silent the entire trip to my home.

Although when two Risen cross our path I get a taste of how Ryan fights. I saw it once before, but it was brief. I was too busy doing my own thing to really worry about his. But now that I'm tucked away in a doorframe again, just as Trent did to me, I get a chance to really see him.

It's impressive.

He has a weapon I've never seen before. It's like brass knuckles with a spike coming out the middle. When he holds his hand up with all of his fingers curled into his palm around the handle, the spike stands up proudly over his middle finger. Like it's flipping the entire world the bird. There are only a few spots on the body that this weapon can be used for an instant kill, but Ryan knows them all. He doesn't hesitate, not one second. He dances around the Risen, looking for the opening he needs, then he strikes like a viper into the eye, the ear. Fast, accurate, brutal. He's like Trent, quick and efficient, but there's something so much more fluid about him and his fight. It's almost like watching a dance.

When he's done, breathing heavily surrounded by a circle of rotted, mutated bodies, I give him a small round of applause. It's faint and frail, the best I can do with the hands I have at the moment, but he smiles and bows theatrically. It's an ugly scene; all death, blood, gore and everything macabre. But there in the middle is this boy. This vibrant, living, breathing, resilient, relentless boy – and he's smiling. At me.

I cannot help but smile back.

When we finally reach my building, I nearly collapse with relief at being there. I hurry up the steps, jostling my arm painfully but unable to stop myself. I want to see if it's okay. If all of my things have disappeared or been destroyed. I can't imagine they've been left untouched. Not with Ryan and probably Trent knowing where I live. Something's bound to have gone missing.

I push inside quickly, Ryan close on my heels. What I see stops my heart. I gasp in shock, unable to understand.

"What?" I whisper to myself.

It's nothing I expected.

It's perfect. Everything is in its place. From my

bike to the water canister to the Hello Kitty bag I keep my veggies in. It's all there. Even the blankets that I usually toss onto my makeshift bed are folded neatly. Like they're waiting for me.

"I came here almost every day," Ryan says quietly from behind me. "I knew where you were, but I always hoped you'd be here when I came in. Or that one day I'd go to open the door and it'd be locked."

"How did you know where I was?" I ask, too scared of him and myself to turn around.

"Trent said he saw a girl taken. A girl with long red hair. That would have been enough to convince me, but then he told me she fought like an animal. That she stabbed a guy and broke his nose." I hear him chuckle softly. "After that, I knew it was you. And I knew that if anyone could get away, it was you."

"So you waited," I whisper.

"And I hoped."

I spin on my heels and I kiss him soundly. I press my body as close to his as my arm will allow and I sigh when his hands slide around me. He'll never know what that means to me. How much it hurts me to hear him say he hoped I'd come back. That someone out there knew I was gone and wanted me back. It's what I wanted while I was trapped; for him to remember me and carry me with him in the wild under the free open sky. I've been alone for too long, been running from those feelings for years and now here they are staring me in the face, straightening my world and waiting for me to come home. I hate it and I love it and when I think of what I wrote on the wall in the Colony, I whimper quietly in the back of my throat. I missed this. This kiss, these hands, this voice that knows my name, this heartbeat clamoring inside his chest, pushing against mine.

Then I whimper in pain as my arm is crushed between us. Ryan releases me immediately, holding me at arm's length.

"I'm sorry, Joss," he mutters, his breathing uneven. "I forgot about your arm. We need to deal with that right now."

I groan, letting my head hang back. "This is gonna suck so bad."

"Sorry," he repeats.

He heads for my bathroom. I'm not surprised when he comes back out with my bottle of vodka.

"Here. Get to work on that. It'll take the edge off. It's still going to hurt, but it will hurt a lot less."

I sniff the open top of the bottle, my lips curling back in disgust. "I've never drank it before."

"I'm a little jealous."

"Good God, why? It smells like acid."

Ryan chuckles. "It'll taste a lot better than the stuff at the markets. Drink too much of what they sell there and you'll go blind."

I cringe at the thought of going to the markets. I'm going to have to, though. How else am I going to get an audience with The Hive? I can't exactly walk up to the door and knock. I'll be shot or shoved into their stables, no questions asked. It's something I need to talk to Ryan about, but not yet. One painful thing at a time and right now my arm has soundly called dibs.

I take a swig of the vodka. It's not bad, not at first. Then the burn hits. I double over, coughing and grabbing at my chest where the heat is coursing through it into my stomach.

"Why?" I gasp, not really sure what I'm asking. Why do people drink this stuff? Why does it hurt so bad? Why are my insides on fire?

"You okay?"

"Ugh!" I groan. I stand up straight, my face frozen in a tortured grimace as the burn just keeps on going. "This is terrible."

Ryan shakes his head. "That's the good stuff. And you'll need more of it than that. Better keep drinking before you lose your nerve."

I glare at him, thinking of the rooftop. The jump. The fall.

"I never lose my nerve."

He silently makes a drinking motion with his hand before crossing his arms over his chest, watching me patiently.

I take three more good, long pulls off the bottle before I hand it back to him. It was easier doing it all at once. I still want to die, though. Ryan stows the bottle back in the bathroom before coming to stand in front of me again. He doesn't say anything, just watches me.

"What?" I ask, feeling antsy being under the microscope.

"Now we wait. It'll hit you soon."

"What's it going to feel like?"

He smirks. "What does drunk feel like? Uh, good, I guess is the best way to describe it. You'll be a little dizzy, feel a little flushed. You might vomit eventually."

I frown. "So it's like being sick."

"Kinda, yeah. But in a good way. You'll laugh more, which will be nice."

"Do you have a problem with my attitude?"

"Asked the girl frowning at me," he retorts, pointing at my furrowed brow. I try to relax it, but I don't know if it works. Ryan grins. "Nah, I like you're attitude, Joss. But I like your laugh too."

29

"You've barely heard it."

"Exactly. I'm looking forward to it."

"Why do you like me, Ryan?" I mumble quietly. "I'm not nice."

"Oh good," he says, taking my shoulders, "it's working." He sits me down on my bed, pressing my back against the wall. I'm glad to be sitting because the room has started to tilt. "You haven't eaten recently, have you?"

"Not for hours and hours and hours."

"This will be fun," he mutters.

He leans in close. I think he's going to kiss me, but his head passes by mine as his fingers get to work on the knot of my sling. When it releases, I'm not ready and the pain explodes through my entire body. I grit my teeth hard, willing myself not to make a sound. He sees it when he sits back.

"Are you okay?"

"Uh huh," I grunt.

"Joss, it's okay to—"

"I said I'm fine."

"Alright."

What happens next is a waking nightmare. Fixing the damage done to my body hurts worse than the damaging did. Tears stream down my face as Ryan methodically cleans, sets and splints my arm. Because the bone pushed through the skin, I'm in danger of getting an infection. I'm also in white hot agony because Ryan had to realign the bone before he splinted it to make sure it heals right.

That. Hurt.

I've never sworn so much in my life. I curse Ryan up and down, sideways, forward and backward, but he never flinches. Never hesitates. He's calm and collected, completely methodical through the entire thing. He ignores the sweat pouring down my forehead, the shaking in my limbs, the tremble in my voice. At one point, I grab onto his shoulder with my good hand and clench down on it with all my strength, but he keeps right on working. I've bruised him, I know it, but he never complains.

When it's done, when I'm shaking with exhaustion, he finally looks up at me. I expect to find pity or sadness, but there's nothing. He's gone numb inside. To do what had to be done, to hurt me to help me, he's tapped out entirely. Based on his skill at cleaning and splinting my arm, this isn't his first time. He's done this over and over again and in order to stay sane, he's gotten good at not feeling it.

I take a deep, shuddering breath then manage a meager grin.

"Thanks," I breathe.

"Ha," he laughs shortly, not sounding at all amused. "I don't think that deserves gratitude."

"It wouldn't heal right if you hadn't done this," I mutter, feeling suddenly too weary to live, "and I'd die without it."

He looks at me long and hard, his expression still carefully blank. I wait, wondering what he's thinking. Eventually I can't take it anymore.

"You wanna take a hit of that vodka with me?"

"Hell yeah," he mutters, already heading for the bathroom.

He sits down beside me, just a breath of space between us, but it's enough. It's enough so that I don't feel overwhelmed with how close he is. That I don't feel boxed in and afraid. It's close enough that I know he's there and the loft doesn't feel so huge. So empty.

He takes a hit off the bottle before handing it over to me. I take a drink as well, this time not minding the burn so much.

"I need to go out and get you something for the infection," he says, sounding as tired as I feel.

"We don't know I have one yet."

"You will," he replies, taking the bottle back and downing another swig. "The world is dirty. Where did it happen?"

"On a roof."

"Do I want to know how?"

"I jumped. It was too far."

He nods silently beside me. We both stare into the distance, passing the bottle back and forth without a word. I look at the wall by the door, the one where he once wrote his address. I wiped it off not long after he did it. Not long after I decided I could stay. Not long after I memorized it.

"How'd you get out?"

It's the million dollar question. It's one I would have asked a long time ago, but Ryan is more patient than I am. It's also a question I don't want to answer because the answer is too ugly. Too real. But if anyone is going to understand it, it's Ryan.

My heart is in my throat, threatening to choke me, but I swallow past it.

"I killed a woman," I tell him hoarsely.

He doesn't answer. He doesn't move. He barely breathes.

"She tried to kill me," I tell him quietly, because I feel compelled to explain. To make him understand. To make sure I understand. "She stabbed my friend. I'm not even sure he's still alive. But then she came at me too and I knew she'd kill me if she got the chance. I knew she'd finish him off when I was gone, so I killed her."

I can hear my heartbeat in my ears, thumping loudly. Painfully. It hurts to breathe.

"It was easy," I whisper.

Ryan clears his throat, then hands me the bottle. "You'll never get over it."

I pause, the bottle at my lips. "Gee, thanks. That's helpful."

"You won't because you're a good person. Because you know it's messed up. That it's wrong. It's been over a year and I'm not over doing it. I know I never will be, but I live with it. Sometimes it even makes me feel better knowing that I can't get over it."

I take a drink, hand the bottle back.

"Why?" I wheeze against the burn.

He takes a long drink. "Because if I hate it, I'm still human, you know? I'm not an animal yet. Not like some of the other people out there."

"I guess that makes sense."

Ryan shrugs, capping the bottle. "Whether it does or it doesn't, it's what works for me. Maybe it will work for you or maybe you'll have to find something else."

"Like what?"

"I don't know, I'm not an expert."

"Maybe I should ask one," I mumble, thinking of The Hive looming in my future and the many killers within its walls. I spin Vin's ring absently, wondering if he's still alive. The ring feels especially heavy on my finger, weighing down my already injured, aching arm.

"What's that?" Ryan asks, eyeing the ring.

"A key."

"To what?"

I sigh heavily. "Probably my own prison."

Tracey Ward

Chapter Four

Ryan leaves to get me something for the infection he's sure is coming. I don't know where he's going because I don't ask, but I have a hunch. A hunch that's been forming since I smelled the soap on his bed. When he comes back with familiar brown bottles, I know for sure.

"How is he?" I ask, unable to stop myself.

Ryan looks at me in surprise. I'm surprised myself because one thing we all know when dealing with Crenshaw is that you don't go blabbing about it to other people. He doesn't want to trade with everyone, doesn't want to be known by everyone, so if you're in his good graces you stay there by zipping your lips.

I grin, feeling awkward breaking the rules. "Is he alright? I usually bring him meat because he refuses to hunt, but... I've been busy lately."

Ryan grins as well, his surprise turning to understanding. "He's good. I'll take him some meat tomorrow."

"Thanks."

"Do you want me to tell him you're home?"

"No," I say immediately. "Don't mention me. I don't want him to know I talked. Take him meat as payment for the medicine. I'll go see him when I'm—I don't know. Not so busy, I guess."

Ryan stops his work with the bottles but he doesn't look at me.

"Are you going back for him? For your friend?"

"Yes," I admit wearily. "I promised I'd come back for all of them."

He looks up, frowning at me. "All of who?"

"My friends inside the Colony."

"You made friends inside the Colony?" he asks skeptically. "As in more than one?"

"You say it like it's impossible," I snap at him.

"Well, you're not exactly…"

"What? What aren't I, Ryan?" I ask sharply, glaring at him.

He grins. "Friendly."

"Oh shut up," I grumble, knowing he's right.

He goes back to arranging my medicines, chuckling to himself. I take my disgusting herbal blends without complaint, promising to continue taking them at regular intervals. Ryan has brought me food to eat as well, and I swear old dry carrots have never tasted so good. They're absolutely dripping with freedom.

"I have to go," Ryan admits reluctantly. "I don't want them to come looking for me."

"Okay," I reply evenly, feeling relieved and anxious at the same time.

There's nothing about Ryan that doesn't bring out contradiction in me. I want him to stay but I don't know how to *be* with him here. I want him to go but I'll miss the feel of him nearby. I hated it the first night I met him, how he confused everything and filled the room nearly to bursting with just his laugh. But now… I don't know for sure. Now I've learned I can be around people, and if I have to be around anyone, I'd rather it was him.

"You'll be okay?" he asks.

I give him a pointed look.

"Right, of course you will. Alright, I'll be back tomorrow."

He rises from beside my bed, backing toward the door.

"So soon?" I ask, surprised. "Isn't that risky?"

He shrugs. "Maybe, I guess. When do you want me to come back?"

Tonight.

"Tomorrow."

He smiles. "You sure?"

"No," I say, shaking my head with a wan smile, "but come back anyway."

He leans down abruptly, taking me by surprise. His lips brush across my forehead once quickly, then, before I can freak out, he's heading for the door.

"Lock this behind me, okay?" he calls to me.

"I will."

He pauses, halfway out the door. His brown eyes find mine, holding onto me for a long, silent moment. He opens his mouth to say something but thinks better of it. Finally he says quietly, "Goodnight, Joss."

"Goodnight, Ryan."

When he's gone, I close my eyes and picture him heading down the stairs, his strange weapon in his hand. He's crossing the street, heading parallel to the park, back toward the building with the wood burning smell and the real mattress and the books in the walls. He'll sleep on the bed with the scattered blankets smelling of soap and sweat. And maybe they'll smell a little of me. A little like Colony soap, harsh laundry detergents, vomit, fear and longing. It'll smell like a caged animal newly released to the wild. Shaking scared, disoriented.

Angry.

***

A week later, Trent shows up at my door.

Alone.

Ryan has been visiting every other day, checking on my arm to make sure infection isn't running rampant. That I haven't turned green. That I'm not jonesing for human flesh. It's a worry you have these days no matter where you got your cut. Open wound means open to the sickness. No exceptions. I'm on full loft lock-down until I'm better healed and I am going out of my mind with boredom. My new favorite past-time? Knife throwing. It won't do you a bit of good with a Risen, but with other people (something I am surrounded by lately), it's a good talent to have.

Too bad I suck at it.

When Trent knocks on my door, I have a knife raised in my right hand. I was ready to throw but now I'm statue still. Waiting.

"Joss."

That's all he says. Just my name. Just once, low and deep in the way he says everything. Even. Methodical. Creepy as balls.

I tip toe to the door, my hand still raised high with the gleaming, sharp blade at the ready. I suddenly wish I had a peephole on my door, though I don't know what it would matter. I know what he looks like. He won't have a weapon showing, even if he intends to murder me.

"What do you want, Trent?" I demand quietly.

"Little pig, little pig, let me in," he whispers.

"Not a chance in Hell, wolf. How do you know

where I live?"

"Is it a secret?"

"I'm not exactly in the phone book."

He chuckles. "Open the door."

"No."

"Ryan sent me."

"Well, I'm sending you right back."

"Why are you so scared of me, Joss?" he asks, sounding like he's mocking me. Like he's soothing a crying baby.

I bristle. "I'm not scared of you. I'm leery of you. Totally different."

"Why are you leery of me?"

"Wouldn't you be?"

When he chuckles again, I tense. His voice is drifting farther away. Farther down the hall *into* the building.

"You're going the wrong way. Exit's to the left, pal!"

"I'm not leaving," he replies calmly. He's farther away now. "I'm looking for another entrance. There are more, aren't there?" His voice is approaching again. Slowly. "Of course there are. There's the fire escape out this window at the end of the hall that will lead up to the roof. Do you have a roof hatch, Joss?"

"It's locked," I snap, hoping it actually is.

"Doesn't matter," he says, his voice drifting the other way now. "There are other ways of getting in there. Don't worry about it. I'll find them."

I don't know what other entrances there may be, but I do know if anyone will find them it's him. Be it Spider-manning his way up the building and through the windows or slithering his way up through my toilet. No matter how the ninja plans on doing it, I'd rather he didn't.

I sigh heavily. I do not put away my knife.

When I open the door, he's standing right there waiting as though he had been the entire time. He's too quiet. Too quick. I'm jealous of it and I hate him for it.

"May I enter?" he drones, bowing gracefully to me, formally asking permission like a friggin' vampire.

"Come in," I say reluctantly, swinging the door open.

"Thought you'd never ask."

He saunters in, scanning the entire loft in one quick assessing glance. I'm pretty sure in that one move he catalogued my entire world, underwear included. And he did it alphabetically.

"What are you doing here?" I ask, never leaving the door. I also leave it open as an invitation to leave.

"I told you, Ryan sent me." He stands in the center of the room, his hands in his pockets. "What made you open the door? I thought you were leery of me."

"I am and I should be. You're shifty." I spin my knife in my hand, just so we both know I have it. "And because you're shifty, keeping you out started to feel like delaying the inevitable. Like a Risen at your door. They're never going away. Eventually you have to make them go."

He grins at me. "I promise not to overstay my welcome."

"You already have."

"That was fast."

"It doesn't take long with me."

He smirks. "Do you know why I like you, Joss?"

"I'm sure I have no idea."

"It's for the same reasons Ryan does." He holds up his hands in innocence. "Our reasons are the same, but our motives are completely different, I promise. I don't see cozying up to someone like you. It'd be like loving a skunk."

"Nice," I deadpan. "Very charming."

He shrugs. "I have as much use for charm as you do. What I mean is, a skunk scares easy. They're solitary. When they don't want you around, they let you know it and they send you home with a reminder for days."

"You make a good point. You're very chatty today, aren't you?" I ask suspiciously.

"I am. It's one of the reasons I like you. I can talk to you. You're not all bravado and bullshit."

"Thank you?" I ask, frowning.

He shakes his head dismissively. "It was an observation. If you want compliments, talk to Ryan. He'll tell you the sun rises and sets in your hair. That your eyes remind him of rain."

My frown deepens. "What does that even mean?"

"I have no idea, but he would understand it and if you heard *him* saying it, you'd understand it too." He grins mischievously at me. It's very Cheshire. Very cat ate the canary. "Ryan has use for charm."

I don't want to talk about Ryan and his charm. Or my eyes or his eyes or anyone's thoughts on either of them. That's a whole mess of crap that I don't understand. I also feel like it's something I cannot and do not want to stop which makes it scary and I hate being scared. But I want it.

It's confusing.

"Why are you here?" I ask, feeling like I'm repeating myself.

Trent approaches me abruptly, reaching for my arm. I jump away from him into the hall, careful not to be trapped. He eyes me blankly.

"I need to look at your arm and report back to Prince Charming," he tells me calmly.

"You're not touching it," I snap. He narrows his eyes at me and I sigh. "I don't even let Ryan touch it. Not since he bandaged it. I'm not... I'm not good at being touched. I'm not good at trusting people."

"You don't say."

"Just go, okay? I'm fine. Thanks so much for stopping by."

He stands in the open doorway, looking out into the hall at me. Finally he gestures to the knife in my hand.

"If I come toward you to leave, are you going to stab me?"

I squeeze my hand reflexively. "Maybe."

"I'll take my chances."

He steps toward me very slowly, very deliberately. I want to stick him. It's instinct for me and I can't turn it off. I can barely stand Ryan in my space. Having someone come at me that I don't trust? Part of me is itching to put the blade in him and drop him to the ground. I don't want to kill another person, that's not what it is. It's survival. It's spending years not having people in my personal space. It's something I felt coiled inside of me in the Colony but I never had a weapon to do anything about it. Nothing more violent than a fork. But standing here now with him advancing on me, his sharp, predators gaze locked on my face, and the means to defend myself? Auto-pilot is begging to come back on and I very nearly slam the blade into his stomach. To the hilt.

"Oooh," he says quietly, watching my eyes. "You're thinking about it. That's good. You don't want to lose that edge. Going soft will get you killed."

I take a quick, deep breath but my voice is rock solid. "Crowding me while I'm armed will get you killed too."

"I'm not worried," he says with that feline grin of his. He steps away, turning his back on me to show just now not worried he is. As he walks down the hall, leaving me standing there with my knife ready and my muscles aching to end somebody, he calls over his shoulder, "You're holding that knife all wrong. I'd have had it in your stomach before you'd ever get it near mine."

***

It's not until a week later that I finally have to explain what I plan to do. I think Ryan and I were both avoiding it; me because I simply didn't want to tell him and have to face his reaction to it, and him because he was so happy to have me back and alive he didn't want to talk about me committing suicide just yet.

During that week, the weight of Vin's ring gets heavier and heavier. After the first week, when I know I've missed the market and it won't come around again for another month, I can barely choke down my meals I'm so riddled with guilt. Letting people in is more painful than I remember. It's not just the pain of watching them die, rise again and having to kill them yourself for the final time. That's manageable. It's this everyday complicated, emotional nonsense that makes me want to cut and run every single day. It has occurred to me more than once to pack up my gear and head for the hills. To leave all of this behind me and forget any of it ever happened. Ryan, Vin, Trent, the Colony, Nats, the kitchen crew, the pumpkin pie. It was all a strange, tasty dream. One I will work for years to forget. But I know from experience that I can and will eventually forget. At least I hope.

"Joss?" Ryan prods, pulling me back to reality. "Lay it on us."

Trent is sitting beside Ryan across from me on the floor. The long lines of the tall windows shine huge rectangles of light into the room around us, casting the boys partially in shadow, partially in light. Trent's eyes watch me intently from the dark and I think it's no accident, the way he's sitting.

"When I was in the Colony," I begin, spinning the ring on my finger nervously. "I made friends with some people. One of them was a pimp from The Hive."

Ryan scowls at me, surprised and obviously annoyed by this information. Trent couldn't care less.

"He was in there with two of the women from their stables. One of them went full native, but the other wanted out just like us. I ended up making some friends in the kitchens too. Eventually, they told me that the people in the Colonies aren't happy with how things are being run. They're locked in, just like I was, and being preached to about keeping the unclean out. Their cleansing process when you go in there is creepy thorough, I can vouch for that. But worst of all, they're separating families. They're doing it to keep people in line, to have a threat to hang over their heads. I think the higher ups must know their people are getting pissed at being locked in and they're trying to keep them under control. Otherwise, why do it?"

Trent nods in silent agreement.

"And these people," Ryan asks, disbelieving, "the angry ones, they want out of the Colonies?"

"Not entirely. They don't want to come live in the

wild. It terrifies them."

"Then where will they go? And how will they break out?"

"How did Joss do it?" Trent asks, his eyes on me.

I don't flinch. "That's not important."

Trent grins slightly, but he doesn't respond. He knows. Not even because Ryan told him, which he might have, but he just knows.

"We'll have to break them out," I tell Ryan. "After that, they want to gain control of the buildings again. Get their freedoms back."

He laughs. "Seriously? They want to stage a coup? And you and I, we're going to break them out? How?"

I'm annoyed he's laughing at me, but I'm grateful he's lumped himself in with me as well. I hadn't hoped for that.

"We won't do it alone."

"No, because that's impossible."

"We need help from The Hive."

His smile disappears. "Now I know you're joking," he says seriously.

I shake my head faintly. "I'm not."

"Joss, that's insane," Ryan says, his voice rising. "You can't work with The Hive. You can't ask for *help* from The Hive."

"I have an in." I hold up my splinted left arm, showing him my finger wearing the ring. "Vin, the guy from The Hive, he gave me this when I left. He said to take it to Marlow, the head of The Hive. He said to tell Marlow that he sent me."

"This is the guy who got stabbed, isn't it?" Ryan asks, his voice going low.

I nod. "He was stabbed because of me. Well, partially. Partly because he was a careless man whore, but also because of me. I owe it to him to go back for him. I owe it to all of them."

"And this guy, this pimp, he thought Marlow would help you if you showed him that ring?"

"No. He was pretty sure it wouldn't work."

Ryan frowns, his face exasperated. "Then why are you even thinking about doing this?"

I don't have a good answer for that. Not a smart one. So I give him the only one I do have.

"Because I made a promise," I say firmly. "I don't do that very often. I'd like to keep it."

"That's honorable," Trent tells me.

Ryan shakes his head at him. "It's stupid is what it is."

"Most honorable things are."

"I need you to take me to the market," I tell Ryan. "I need to go there and make contact with someone from The Hive so I can try to get an audience with Marlow."

"The market isn't the place to do it," Trent tells me.

My shoulders sag, deflating with my meager hopes. "Then where? The market is the only place I know of where you all come together."

"Really?" he asks, his eyebrows raised.

"Oh man," Ryan mutters. He runs his hand over his face quickly, looking annoyed. "Don't."

"Are you talking about the fights?" I ask. "The Risen fights?"

Trent nods solemnly. "There are more members, more high members, of The Hive at the Underground than you'll ever find in the markets. If you go to the market, you'll only get the run around and end up owing a favor to some ugly people who got you nowhere. You want Marlow or one of his inner circle, you have to go to the Underground."

"Can you take me there?"

"Yes."

"No," Ryan says firmly.

"Why not?" I demand.

"Because this is stupid, Joss. This whole entire thing is crazy. What are you hoping to gain from talking to Marlow? His help? He won't help you. They're not a helpful bunch."

"I know that," I say indignantly.

"Then what are you thinking?"

"I'm thinking I have to try!" I shout, losing myself. "I'm thinking I care for once and I want to help people. Vin and Nats, they're like me, Ryan. They'll die in a place like that. It will break them just like it would have broken me. And I care so that bothers me and it sucks but the switch has been flipped and you flipped it so you can't tell me to undo what's already been done."

Ryan stares at me in the falling light, his face looking strong and golden in the amber glow. He's changed everything and he knows it. He can hate this plan all he wants, but he has to understand that if I'm going to care about him, I'm going to care about others as well. It may get me killed, just as I knew feeling anything for him could, but it doesn't make it any less worth it. I can see it in his eyes, what Nats warned me about. It's harder to live than it is to survive, but he's worth it. Going to sleep knowing I tried for the others, even if I'm sleeping in the stables of The Hive, will be worth it.

"I'll take you there," Ryan tells me quietly. Reluctantly. "Give me two weeks and I'll take you."

"Two weeks? Why not tonight?"

He snorts, shaking his head. "You can't go with that splint on. They get off on weakness and you'll have to at least be able to pretend your arm isn't useless. Besides, I haven't been there in a while. I can't just show up one night with a girl no one's ever seen before on my arm, asking to talk to the boss."

"You've been to the fights before?"

"A time or two."

I turn to Trent. "You too?"

He simply nods.

"And they know you down there?"

"Yeah," Ryan says, smiling sadly. "They know me there."

Chapter Five

A week later, while Ryan and Trent show their faces in the Underground on the regular, I make a visit to Crenshaw. It's a little scary going out with my arm in the splint and the Risen population still bloated from the fall of the Colony, a Colony I have now lived inside of, but I'm going stir crazy in my apartment. I have to get out and I have to face Crenshaw.

When I go to my wall of weapons to pick something out, I nearly burst into tears. There, hanging in its home, is my ASP. It must have been here this entire time, I just never noticed it because I didn't need to, but now that I see it I'm nearly crying with relief. After Trent saw me taken he must have told Ryan where it happened. Maybe Trent told him that I'd lost my weapon or maybe he found it on accident, who knows. The important thing is that it's here, right where I need it.

And I do need it. The Risen population is still high, still an ongoing problem reminding me of the old days. They shuffle and bumble down the streets, through alleyways and into everything. I stand in my doorway for a bit watching and remembering as they walk into each other. Into the remnants of cars. Into old sign posts. It'd be comical if it weren't such a pain. If it didn't remind me of the worst times of my very, very worst case scenario life.

I manage to use my ASP to take down three on the way to the woods. My breathing hitches as I run toward them. I can't afford to be scared but I can't trust myself either, not with this jacked up arm. I struggle to stay calm, to be numb and smart as I work through them. Each one drops with a fractured skull and a hit to the temple just for good measure. Injured or no, it never hurts to be thorough. Only this does, it hurts. Physical activity of any kind, especially running or bashing in skulls, makes my arm throb to a painful rhythm.

When I reach the woods and call out for Crenshaw, I'm shocked to see him emerge entirely from the shadows. He walks right up to me, staff ever in hand, and wraps his arms tightly around me without a word.

"Cren," I say awkwardly, my mouth pressed into the hood of his robe, "do you know you're hugging me?"

He pulls back, still holding onto my shoulders. His face is very nearly beaming. "Athena, I'd thought you lost for the ages."

I smile despite my discomfort at his proximity. "No, I'm still here."

"Thank the stars for small favors," he says, gesturing to the blue, afternoon sky. "Come, sit with me awhile and tell me of your adventures to the great beyond."

He leads me through the bushes toward his hut, past the traps and snares meant to deter and murder anyone dumb enough to trespass here.

"There's not much to tell, really."

"They took you," he says frankly, his face firm. Annoyed.

"Yes."

"The rogues," he grumbles as we enter his hut. He sits me down across from him at his small table. "They knew not with whom they were dealing. Athena! Goddess of War and Vengeance."

"Amen to that."

"How did you escape?"

I hesitate, unsure how I want to handle this. I didn't want to admit to Ryan what I'd done and I can't imagine telling the story to Crenshaw. He might be proud, which I don't know if I'll particularly like, or he could be angry with me. Again, not something I'd like.

"I heeded wise words," I tell him meaningfully. "I kept my wits sharp and luck favored the prepared."

"Ha!" Crenshaw exclaims excitedly, clapping his hands together once. "Wonderful. Well done, my dear. I knew you were not a lost cause."

"Thank you," I say, not really sure it's a compliment. Maybe it's just an observation. Stupid Trent.

"Your arm," Crenshaw says suddenly, his demeanor becoming sedated. "Have you been caring for it? Do you need anything for the pain or infection?"

"No, thank you. I've been taking medicines for it."

He scowls at me. "From whom? Not one of those Charlatan's in the markets, I hope."

"No, Cren. From you."

Crenshaw stares at me for a lone moment before nodding sagely. "The boy."

"Yes," I reply, feeling nervous. I'm breaking a rule here by mentioning a Lost Boy in his presence. We never speak specifics and I've just gotten very, very specific.

"He's a good one, that lad. Stay close to him."

"Really?" I ask, shocked. "I thought I was supposed

to avoid the company of men."

Crenshaw nods again, watching me. "There are few good men left in this world of wraiths, devils and fools, my child. Should you find one, you'd be an idiot to walk away. And you, Athena," he says, heavily, "are no idiot."

"I don't know about that. I've been pretty stupid lately."

He waves my protest away dismissively. "Youth!" he cries, as though that one word explains away every complication in my entire world.

And who knows? Maybe it does.

***

Two nights later I'm scared to death by a pounding on my door. It's not frantic, but it's loud and insistent. I wrap my blanket around me, hiding the shorts and threadbare t-shirt I'm sleeping in, and run for the door.

"Who is it?" I whisper into the crack, feeling ridiculous. I'm not used to visitors. All I know is that if their answer is '*Ughhhhh*', they are not coming in.

"Joss, it's us," Ryan replies weakly.

I quickly lift the board off the door and fling it open. There they stand, Trent and Ryan, leaning against each other. They're both covered in blood. Some of it is way too dark to be theirs. To be human.

"What the hell happened to you two?"

"Can we come in and tell you that?" Ryan asks impatiently. "My leg is killing me."

I step aside to let them pass, but I eye Trent hard as I do. "Why does his leg hurt?"

"You ask that like you think I had something to do with it."

"Did you?"

Trent chuckles quietly. I get no other answer.

I slam the door, dropping the board over it again. Trent drops Ryan down carefully in the middle of the room. He collapses back, breathing hard with his arm thrown over his eyes. I watch as he flexes his right leg back and forth, a grimace etched around his mouth.

"What happened?" I ask again, my tone softening. I go to step closer, to kneel down to help him, but Trent comes straight at me. I instinctively back up against the door, my eyes darting toward my weapons wall as his shadow moves through the dark loft.

"Easy," he says calmly. "I was just leaving."

"What about Ryan?"

"You'll play nurse to him better than I will. The gang can't know he's fighting freelance. I've gotta get back and tell everyone he's spending the night with a pro named Freedom."

I frown, confused and freaked out. "Is that where he was? With a whore?"

Ryan lifts his head off the ground to glare at me. "You think a girl did this to me?"

"Why not?" I ask with a shrug. "I could."

He laughs, dropping his head hard against the wood floor. "Touché."

"You're not really a girl, though," Trent tells me.

Ryan laughs again.

"Wow, Trent, thanks for that," I say sarcastically.

"I mean, you look like one right now, for sure," he says, his eyes falling down my body exposed by the drooping blanket. I snatch it up closer around myself, glaring at him as he grins. "But your average girl couldn't survive like you have."

"Is that a compliment?"

He shakes his head, stepping closer and forcing me away from the door. "Nope. Not everything is a compliment or an insult, Joss. Sometimes things just are what they are." He steps outside into the hall. "Take care of our boy. I'll see you two in the morning."

"That guy is…" I begin, dropping the board across the door yet again. I don't know what else to say. He's not annoying, but he's not fun either.

"He's Trent," Ryan mumbles, still flexing his leg.

"Exactly."

And suddenly Trent's parting philosophy lesson makes a world of sense. I decide he's annoying after all.

"So what happened?" I ask Ryan, plopping down on the floor beside him.

He lowers his arm, giving me a good look at his face in the moonlight. It's covered in small cuts and tiny abrasions. He's bleeding a little everywhere. Walking through the streets like this, casting out that living, bleeding scent, was insanely dangerous. It makes me grateful for the dark undead blood splattered over his shirt and coat. At least he had some camouflage.

"I fought in the Underground tonight."

"You've done it before, haven't you?"

"Yeah."

"How often?"

He looks away, staring straight up at the ceiling. He looks exhausted, beaten. I have a hard time believing that this is what winning looks like, but he's still alive so it must be.

"Not as often as my brother. He did it a lot. He was kind of a legend."

"Is that how people know you there?"

"Partly. I haven't fought since just before he died. He didn't want me to. He fought for our gang as a way of making money. To earn favors from other gangs. It's dangerous though."

"Yeah, I imagine. You're fighting Risen for fun. What if you'd been bitten?" I look over his body, finding more black tar blood as I search. "What if some of this has gotten inside you?"

"That's not why it's dangerous."

"Ryan, you could die. It's a big, big part of it."

I feel panic begin to well inside of me as I look down at him, busted and bleeding. There's Risen gore all over him, more of it by the minute it seems like, and I'm flashing back to all the times I've had to put a gun to someone's head and lay them down just before the fever took over. Just before they stopped being them and started eating me.

I reach for his shirt, tugging it up toward his face. "We have to get you out of these clothes and cleaned up. You can't sit in them acting like the blood isn't seeping into you."

"Whoa, Joss, slow down," he says, trying to stop my hands.

I won't have it. I slap his hands away and yank on the collar of his shirt, pulling him up into a sitting position. His face is close to mine, his breath on my skin and the sheen of his blood is reflecting bright in the moonlight. In my watery eyes. I yank on the hem of the shirt, pulling it up forcefully. This time he lets me. He puts his arms over his head and lets me carefully peel it over his face, taking extreme care not to let the outside of the saturated shirt touch his vulnerable, open skin.

When I toss it aside, already dreaming of the fire I'll burn it in, I feel his eyes on me. Watching. Worrying. I refuse to meet them. Instead, I look over his now exposed chest, arms, stomach and shoulders, searching for any kind of cut that could have left him exposed. But there's nothing. He's perfect. He's safe.

He's an idiot.

I sit back hard on my heels. My eyes are still burning, but I let him see.

"Never again," I tell him firmly.

"I'm fine. You can see it, I'm fine," he says calmly, smiling and reaching for my hand.

I jerk it away. "This time. This time you're fine. But what about next time? People die doing this, don't they?"

"Yeah," he admits quietly, his smile gone. "They do all the time."

"Never again," I repeat.

He sighs as he runs his hand over his hair. "I have to. It's what you need to get to The Hive."

"We'll find another way."

"There is no other way."

"You're not worth it, Ryan," I snap. He looks at me, surprised by my tone. "No matter what I need, you're not worth it. You can't come bursting in here, scribbling your gibberish all over everything, making me give a crap, then go out there and die. You *can't*."

"Hey," he breathes, reaching for my hand again.

And again, I jerk it back.

"Hey," he repeats, this time forcefully. Like a scolding. "Give me your hand, Joss."

I let out a rough breath, then try to smile at him weakly. "Just because I don't want you to die doesn't mean I want you to touch me."

"You're a massive pain, do you know that?"

I reach out, taking his one hand in both of mine. It feels less claustrophobic this way, having him pressed between my palms instead of being clenched inside his.

I can handle this.

"I know that," I agree, staring at his long, beaten fingers. "We need to clean you up."

He stands, then tugs on my hands, trying to pull me up as well. I stay stubbornly seated, looking up at him.

"Who's the whore?"

"What?" he laughs.

"Freedom. You guys didn't make her up, did you? She's real."

He sighs, looking uncomfortable. "Yeah, she's real."

"Who is she?"

"She's a girl my brother was… friendly with."

"She was his girl?"

Ryan shakes his head. "I don't think so. Not really. But he never paid her. I told you, he was a legend in the Underground. This girl really liked him. Her and a lot of other girls."

"Ugh," I groan, finally standing.

"Hey, it's one of the perks. You get good at it, the women start flocking to you."

I point my finger at his mangled face. "Never again!"

He laughs all the way to the bathroom.

I sit on the closed toilet and watch him get cleaned up. I offer to help but he waves me away, claiming he's done it plenty on his own. I believe him.

"How is becoming a Risen not the dangerous part of fighting?"

Ryan hesitates, the alcohol soaked rag hovering over a particularly nasty cut on his face.

"The dangerous part is being good at it," he says quietly. He presses the rag to his skin, flinching slightly. "I got in the ring a few times, but it was never anything official."

"By 'official' do you mean being owned by the gang?" I ask, thinking of Nats and Breanne.

"Yeah. They wanted me to fight for them too, but Kev wouldn't let me. I still got noticed, though. I got offers from other gangs to join up with them."

"To fight for them."

"Yeah."

"You know what I just realized?"

Ryan smirks as he dabs at another spot of blood on his face. "That being a fighter is close to being a prostitute?"

I frown at him, worrying he's a mind reader. "No. I just realized I don't know the name of your gang."

"Do you want to?"

"Is it bad if I do?"

"No," he chuckles. "It's the Hyperions. It's Greek for one of the Titans. He was the father of the sun, the moon and the dawn."

I snort. "So you're a humble bunch?"

Ryan smirks sideways at me. "It's not as impressive as it sounds. He got it on with his sister to have them."

"Sick!"

"Yeah. But we didn't exactly pick the name. The building we're in used to be a theater. It was called the Hyperion."

"Original."

"Judgmental," he says, pointing at me.

"It's rude to point."

"Pot and the kettle and all that," he mutters, dabbing ointment on his fingertips and applying it to his face.

I shrug. "I can't help it. I was raised by wolves."

"Wolves have better manners."

"You hate wolves!" I protest.

"I hate *a* wolf," he corrects, "and he probably still has better manners than you."

I kick him in the shin. Not hard, but it's enough to jostle him and his responding laugh is short lived as it turns into a grunt of pain. I've made him slip, digging his finger into a cut on his face.

"I'm sorry," I say hastily, springing up to stand beside him. "Let me see."

He lets me stand in front of him, dropping his hands down to his sides as I rise up on my toes to look.

"Do you want me to finish it?" I ask, my breath rebounding off his face back at me. I hadn't realized I was standing so close. I meet his eyes and take a deep, calming breath. He's staring at me, watching me. He's patient, but he's tense. "Ryan?"

"Yeah?"

"Do you want to kiss me?" I whisper.

He nods slowly, his eyes never leaving mine.

"Then why don't you?"

"Every time I go to touch you," he says softly, "you pull away. I don't want to crowd you. I don't want you to run."

I reach down with my right hand, taking hold of his. I move it until it sits heavy and warm on my hip. He follows my lead, pressing his other hand on the opposite side of my waist.

"There, see? You're touching me and I'm still here."

"This time," he points out.

"I know. I'm a pain."

"So I've heard."

He kisses me softly, his hands pulling me closer to him. He's careful of my arm this time. He pulls my hips flush with his but leans over me with his upper body. He's holding me and hovering over me and I feel weightless and strange. And warm. His kiss, his breath, courses through me the way the vodka did, burning and churning into my stomach. His fingers find the edge of my thin t-shirt. They slip under, scorching across my skin. I start to feel anxious and so much more. So many things that I don't understand.

I pull away.

Ryan takes his hands away, smiling that crooked smile of his and just like that, the heat fades. I can breathe again.

"We should go to bed," I breathe, trying to bring myself down. To remind myself I'm alright.

Ryan stares are me, surprised.

I swat at him. Hard. I'm not good at being playful. "Not like that and you know it."

"I know," he admits, grinning. "I know what you mean. We should get to sleep."

When we step out of the bathroom, Ryan immediately heads for the door. He lays down slowly beside it, still being careful with his right leg.

"Goodnight," he calls softly, settling in.

I hesitate, unsure. I don't know what I want. Or what he wants. Or what I can handle.

"Ryan, you can—"

"No," he says gently, turning his head to look at me. "I'm good here."

I sigh, feeling relieved. "Do you want a blanket?"

"Do you have one to spare?"

"No, but I'll give it to you anyway."

He chuckles. "That's alright, Joss. I've slept without one before. It won't kill me."

I pad across the room, carrying the blanket with me.

Ryan looks up at me, watching me as I drape it over him.

I grin faintly. "And it won't kill me to share."

"You sure about that?"

I shrug. "Only one way to find out."

Chapter Six

I do not die. I don't exactly sleep, either. Ryan snores. I didn't know this until now because the last time we had a slumber party I kicked him out before anyone fell asleep. He had to go. He was being a dick, asking questions and wanting answers. Who does that?

We expected to see Trent in the morning, but as it drags on into the afternoon, we get worried. Well, I get worried. Ryan says it's no big deal. I suck at this, the worrying and not worrying. Knowing when it's needed, when it's expected and when it's useless but you do it anyway. Exhausting. When it was just me, I didn't have to deal with this crap. I have Ryan to thank for that and I remind myself to kick him in the shins again the next chance I get.

What we do for now is go hunting. I'm out of meat so I know Crenshaw must be too because I'm his sole supplier.

"What do you want to go for?" Ryan asks as we make our way toward the park.

"Shouldn't we hunt somewhere else? Somewhere farther away from your home?"

He shakes his head, rolling his neck and shoulders. His back must be killing him from sleeping on the hard floor all night.

"Nah, there have been roundups around the other hunting grounds."

My stomach flips at the thought of the Colonists. "Are they still swarming the watering holes too?"

"Not as much."

"Have you seen them?"

He scans the roads, his face blank. "Yeah, I've seen them."

I try to smile at him, to reassure him, I think? But I don't really get why I'm doing it, so I stop.

"You okay?"

"I got out," I say, trying to sound solid. Like with the smile, I fail. "I'm great."

What I am is feeling guilty. It's been too long since I made it out of the Colony. I'm sure at this point Vin and Nats think I either betrayed them or The Hive killed me on sight. Is it too jacked up to hope they think I'm dead?

"We'll go back for them, Joss."

I nod my head but I don't say a word because that's all it is. Words. None of it gets us anywhere. None of it brings us closer to where we need to be in order to free them. It's all I can think about every day, even when I'm trying hard not to. When I'm laughing with Ryan and telling myself it'll be okay, I can feel it gnawing at me that it's not. That I'm failing. But I won't sacrifice him for it either. I won't ask him to fight for me.

"There has to be another way," I mutter to myself.

"And we'll find it. I promise."

We've entered the woods and I stop, staring into the darkness beyond the trees. Part of me knew already but I didn't want to do it. I didn't want to break the rules any more than I already have, but I have to because he's my last hope. My last chance at being better than I or Vin ever really were made to be.

"Gandalf."

Ryan frowns at me, following my stare. "What?"

"Crenshaw," I say, looking up at him. "We have to ask Crenshaw."

"Ask him what? To help us?" he asks dubiously. "Unless he's a real wizard and knows how to summon us a dragon, I don't think he can do much for us."

"But he knows things. He knows people. Maybe he knows someone who can help."

"Someone other than The Hive," Ryan agrees, looking into the woods again. "It's worth a shot."

"Let's get a kill first, make sure we have meat to bring him. I worry about his diet."

"People didn't eat meat before the sickness came and they were just fine," Ryan reminds me, falling in step beside me as we venture deeper into the woods.

"I know. I just… I worry about him. I don't want him to get frail, I guess."

Ryan nods in understanding. "He's alone, like you. You want to make sure he's strong enough to fend for himself."

"Yeah, maybe," I mutter.

I'm not sure if he's right but I'm not sure if he's wrong either. The basic fact is that I worry about Crenshaw. I always have. Even before Ryan, people were still with me. I hadn't really noticed before because Crenshaw made it so simple. So black and white, easy to understand. I've always known what he wants from me and what I want from him. With Ryan, it's so much gray. So much I don't get and can't categorize.

When we hunt for rabbit and squirrel, what we get are Risen. Lots of them. There are so many more in the woods than I remember seeing and it sends my stomach straight through to the ground. Ryan is less effected, telling me this is how it's been since the Colony collapse. That it got worse after I left as more filtered down here into the heart of the city. As we close in on three of them, I worry about Ryan's cuts, his aching leg, his stiff shoulders and my busted arm.

"Do you have your ASP?" he asks, flanking the Risen on the left and gesturing for me to do the same on the right.

"Yeah, of course. Thanks for that, by the way."

He grins. "No problem. I'll handle two, you take the third."

"Got it."

My Risen is a beauty. All gray tissue sagging slowly off the face like pizza dough in a hot room. The left eye socket is dropping down over the bone, exposing black muscle tissue that's long past useful and the sagging skin over the top of the eye is probably the only thing holding the bulging eyeball in the socket. I have the morbid desire to lift that flesh and see if I'm right. To see if the eye slips out and dangles down, swinging like a pendulum.

When I hear a grunt from Ryan followed by the moist squish of his spike going into decomposed skin, I snap out of it. I get to work. I swing my right arm across my body, then snap it back out, basically backhanding the Risen in the face with the steel tip of my ASP. It makes a loud crunch, sending a spray of skin and black blood arching into the bushes. The head is snapped back hard and before it can try to right itself, I reverse my momentum and bring the ASP back the way it came. This time I make contact with the side of the skull, right in the sweet spot of the temple. The meatbag drops to the dirt - done.

I've hardly exerted myself, but when I look at Ryan, I'm breathing quickly and grinning.

"How messed up is it that I missed that?" I ask him, not even caring what his answer is.

My injured arm aches but there's so much strength coursing through my veins, it doesn't matter to me. This is so much better than sewing or baking. I'd give up all the pumpkin pie in the world for this feeling. To know I'm strong. Effective. Meaningful. I was nothing in there. Inside the Colony, I was just a body doing a duty. Washing dishes or making a bed. That's not me.

I spin my ASP in my hand, loving the tensile power inside of it, power given to it by my hand. Without me, it's just a piece of steel. Without it, I'm just a broken girl running for her life. Together, we're deadly.

Ryan smiles. "I don't think it's messed up at all."

I nod to his knuckles. "What is that? Did you make it?"

He flexes his fingers, looking at the spike along his knuckles. "Kevin did. He made it for in the arena."

"In the Underground?"

"Yeah."

"It's cool," I tell him admiringly.

He shrugs, looking uncomfortable. "It's better than nothing. Let's get that meat you wanted and go see the wizard."

When we finally manage to bag a couple of rabbits, we start to head back toward Crenshaw's.

"I should do it alone."

He frowns down at me. "Why?"

"He likes me."

"He likes me too," Ryan insists, sounding offended.

"He likes me more."

"What are you? Two years old? It's not a competition. I'm sure daddy loves all his kids the same."

"But I'm special."

"Why? Cause you're a girl? Get over yourself, Joss. I'm going with you."

I want to hit him for trivializing how hard it's been to do this on my own being a girl surrounded by Lost Boys, Colonists and Risen. It's been a nightmare, and honestly, being around people again has its pros and cons too. I can't exactly say it's hands down a better deal than what I had before. It's different, sure, but is it better? I feel annoyed more often, that's about all I know. Like right here, right now.

Annoyed.

"Whatever, let's go."

I turn my back on him instead of hitting him or yelling at him. I feel like that's a sure sign that my social skills are improving.

We reach the edge of Crenshaw's property and pause, scanning the trees.

"You want to knock or should I?" Ryan asks.

"Just do it."

He chuckles. "You are seriously a sore loser."

"I haven't lost anything!"

"Athena?" Crenshaw calls.

"Nothing but your temper," Ryan whispers in my ear, his breath tickling my hair across my neck.

I shiver, shoving him away as I try not to smile.

"I saw that," he mumbles.

"Shut up."

"Ah, Athena," Crenshaw says happily, emerging from the shadows like mist the way he loves to do. "I thought that was you." He looks Ryan up and down briefly. "And you've brought young Helios with you."

I turn to ask Ryan who the hell Helios is, but my words die in my throat. He's down in the grass on one knee, his head bowed.

"Master Crenshaw," he intones deeply.

Crenshaw grins affectionately, waving his hand to him. "Rise, rise, my boy. As you've brought Athena with you, I assume this is to be a social call. No need for such ceremony."

Ryan stands beside me. I stare at me in amazement. "What was that?"

"Shh," he shushes me. "Master Crenshaw, we seek your council."

"Ah, so then it is not entirely a social call."

"No, sir."

"Well, come, my children. Come. You'll sit at my hearth and tell me your troubles."

We follow silently and carefully behind Crenshaw as he leads us through his maze of traps. I'm bursting with questions about what the bowing and 'Master' bit was about, but I lock it up for now. Talking to Crenshaw, especially about real issues, is a delicate thing. Some days you get sharp moments of a man well aware he's living in an apocalypse. Other days, you get the wizard who wants to show you his latest trick of turning water into wine. It's not wine. It's not even grape juice. It's water with mashed up grapes in it, seeds, skins and all. But you drink it because you'll hurt his feelings otherwise and if there's one thing you never do, it's piss off a wizard.

He seats us at his small table inside his hut, Ryan actually on his bed with his long legs tucked up nearly into his chest. We both pass on whatever brew he has going on the stove that wreaks of onions because that's probably what it is, boiling onions, and we offer him a share of our kill in exchange for his advice.

"What knowledge do you seek?" he asks us seriously, his large round eyes scanning both our faces.

Ryan glances at me quickly, looking anxious. This is where it could go well or very wrong. You never know.

I clear my throat. "Helios and I," I begin, feeling like an idiot, "are looking to free the other souls I was imprisoned with."

Crenshaw's face falls in shadow. It's as though the light of the entire world has been sucked from it and the only thing left besides the darkness is the burning fire in his eyes.

"Those zealots," he says quietly, his voice trembling slightly, "have been a menace since the start. I have seen countless souls ensnared in their nets. Countless bodies tossed carelessly within their chariots to be their slaves. To work their fields, tend their livestock. Fatten their King. But the day I knew they'd taken you," he reaches out with his warm, worn hand and rests it gently on top of mine. I tense, doing everything I can to keep my hand there. To sit still and not offend him. I can feel Ryan's eyes heavy on me, on my hand, and the weight of his stare makes it so much worse. "It broke my heart, Athena."

I freeze, staring at him in surprise. I'm surprised by his sad voice, by his angry eyes, but most importantly I'm surprised that it's all for me.

"It did?" I whisper.

"Of course. You are my bellatrix."

"Like in Harry Potter?" Ryan mumbles.

I kick him under the table.

"What does that mean, Cren?"

He laughs, squeezing my hand before mercifully

releasing it. "Your Latin is atrocious! It is a woman warrior. You are a Valkyrie, Athena. Defeating the devils that have escaped Hell's gates."

"I'm not exactly doing it alone," I chuckle nervously, feeling both of their eyes on me.

"No, you're right. You have Helios to help you. I must say that this," Crenshaw gestures between Ryan and I, "is right. It is as it should be. You've fought valiantly, my dear, but there's no shame in accepting help. And Helios, he can help you."

I glance quickly at Ryan, feeling my checks burn with that irritating flush of embarrassment. He smiles smugly at me.

"I know that," I grumble, feeling my ASP against my thigh and the press of the splint on my injured arm, both of which wouldn't be there if it weren't for him. *I* might not be here if it weren't for him and Trent. I'm starting to owe a lot to a lot of people and I'm thinking that debt is another thing I lived without before all of this started. It's also something I have to sink deeper into.

I level my gaze on Crenshaw, stowing my doubts, my girly blushes, and getting down to business.

"I'll need more help than just Helios here," I tell him, jutting my thumb at Ryan. "I've considered going to The Hive, but—"

Crenshaw leaps from his chair, his staff tossed aside carelessly. I have no idea where he got it from, maybe he conjured it from air and rage, but there's a long gleaming dagger suddenly in his hand.

It's pointed at my face.

"You will not," he says, his voice sounding cavernous and strange, "talk about The Hive in my house."

Chapter Seven

Ryan and I are on our feet immediately, instinct kicking in. We're whipping out our weapons before we can even think. Crenshaw pauses, looking from one weapon to the other, his breathing erratic.

"Master Crenshaw," Ryan says calmly, as though he's not holding the Punch of Death pointed at the guy, "we have no quarrel with you. We never have. We want no violence. Can we all be calm? May we stow our weapons and sit again as friends?"

It's nice to know it's not only me. That I'm not the only one who has to slip into character like I'm reading from King Arthur's diary in order to talk to this guy. He watches Ryan for several long, tense moments before nodding his head and taking his seat.

"Please, sit. I apologize for my outburst. My tempers, they flare at the mention of the Zealots but they burn with fire eternal when I'm forced to think of… the others." Crenshaw takes a deep breath as we sit down again, both of us a little further back from the table than we were before. "You mustn't go to them. Promise me."

Ryan and I glance at each other, unsure. I have no desire to break a promise to Crenshaw but if all else fails, I made a promise to the people in the Colony as well. If I'm not careful, I'll end up betraying someone's trust.

"Why, Cren?" I ask him gently. "What are you so against us going to The Hive?"

He closes his eyes, takes a deep breath. "Can you not speak that name in this building? It is my home. My sanctuary." When he opens his eyes to look at me they're tired and sad. "They have taken so much already. I do not care for them to ruin this as well."

"Of course, yeah," I agree, not understanding entirely. But I understand enough. I understand having a home and defending it at all costs. I understand having it taken. Invaded.

"We don't want to go to them," Ryan tells Crenshaw. His eyes are still watching the old man closely. His weapon is still in place on his hand. "We were hoping you could advise us on how to gather people together. To get more help. We could try to rally the gangs, but they don't play well together. Not in a fight."

Crenshaw nods sagely. "Each would wonder what was in it for them."

"Exactly. There'd be so much fighting with each other, we'd never get around to fighting the Colonies. It's why we wanted to go to the largest of the gangs, because they're already united, but," Ryan glances at me quickly, his face unreadable, "we're pretty sure we wouldn't want to pay their price."

"Indeed you would not," he agrees softly. He looks at Ryan with eerily sharp eyes. Eyes that remind me of Trent. That feel too lucid to be my Gandalf the Gray. "Never take her to them. Never let them see her. Women in The H—" He sighs forcefully. "It's no place for women. Especially women like her."

I frown, annoyed that I'm obviously being

discussed as though I'm not sitting right here.

"What do you mean, 'women like her'?" I demand.

"You lost someone to them," Ryan says sadly.

Crenshaw nods.

"To who?" I ask. "To The—to them?"

They ignore me again. I've gone full Casper.

Crenshaw nods. "She was her age. Just as bright. Just as beautiful." He grins faintly. "Just as rough around the edges."

Ryan smiles. "It's part of the beauty."

"The greatest part."

"I'm sorry about your daughter." Ryan says, obviously gleaning more from this conversation than I am. What daughter?

"Don't be sorry for me. Just do a better job protecting her than I did."

"I swear it."

"Good lad."

"What the hell?" I mutter, looking back and forth between them.

They wouldn't hear me with Ouija board.

Crenshaw rises from the table slowly. It's as though his outburst has drained him of everything he had. He's hunched slightly, his movements labored. I have to remind myself that as spry, lively and crazy as he seems, he is an old man. He's got a lot of life under his belt and it's not just bones that get tired.

He goes to a wooden box about the size of a toolbox sitting at the foot of his bed. After digging around silently, he pulls out a large piece of worn, white paper. I'm waiting anxiously to see what this is. It could be anything. A spell book. A nude drawing of Tom Hanks. A cheat sheet to the 2009 SATs. Or something far more disturbing like a nude drawing of himself or a detailed chart monitoring his bowel movements. One never knows.

What he actually does lay out on the table both startles and amazes me.

It's a map of Neverland. A hand-drawn, near perfection, detailed map of the Seattle area. Not as it was, because who cares? This is a map of what the city is today. Instead of zip codes, the city is broken up by gang territories. The stadiums are labeled as what they really are – Colonies. I eagerly search the outer edges to the south, looking to see if Cren knows exactly where the third Colony lies, but there's nothing. Just a drawing of the shoreline with a topless mermaid out in the water, waving at me.

"Whoa," Ryan breathes, stowing his spike hand under the table and leaning forward over the map.

Crenshaw smiles at him happily, his mood shifting dramatically. He's proud and pleased to see Ryan so into his work. Excitement is written all over both of their faces.

"It is incomplete," Crenshaw warns. He spreads it flat with gentle, soothing hands. "I shouldn't be showing it to you, Helios. Other gangs, other tribes, would be angry to know I'd shown you where their hideouts lie. But I have faith in you. I trust in your trueness."

"Thank you, Master Crenshaw," Ryan says with a small smile. He looks so happy. Flattered by the old guy's admiration and I realize I'm not the only one who grew up without a dad. Who feels that missing piece of me.

"I believe I have the names of each of the tribes correct, but of course I'm unsure as to what the true names of the Colonies are."

"C-92," I deadpan, pulling my eyes away from Ryan's smile. I wipe my sweating palms on my pants before pointing to the football stadium. Next I point to the baseball stadium right next door. "G-11. The one in the southeast is somewhere along the water but I don't know where. The people I talked to didn't either. It's G-35."

They stare at me in shock. I don't know if they're surprised I remembered the names or that I know them at all. I have a brief, paranoid and horrifying thought that they'll think I'm a spy. That I didn't 'escape' the Colony at all but that I was released to... what? Be socially awkward with a hot guy and help an old lunatic finish his map quest?

"Where were you held?" Ryan asks.

He's looking at me, I can feel it. I keep my eyes trained on the table.

"The MOHAI," I reply curtly.

"The what?"

I point to the spot on Cren's map. The small area tucked in the harbor that felt a million miles away from here but now looks so close. Too close. And too small to house so many people. Too small to house a person like Vin.

"It was here. In the old museum building. I can't remember what MOHAI stands for, but it was Colony A-36."

Crenshaw quickly whips out a charcoal pencil from his box of goodies and begins filling in the information I've given him.

"Why did they name them like that?" Ryan asks, watching Crenshaw's simple, slanting handwriting scrawl over the pages. I expected something more somehow. Old English flourishes or Latin. Maybe

Aramaic. These chicken scratches annoy me. "It seems so cold compared to what they're always spouting on the billboards or over their intercoms."

"Everything about them is a lie," Crenshaw mutters.

"It's to confuse people." I point vaguely to the MOHAI. "The people in the building where I was held are pulled from all of the other Colonies. It's what I told you about breaking up families. Every one of those people has someone in another Colony somewhere. Someone they care about. They all have something to lose."

Ryan nods. "Makes sense. It's a good way to control people. But why did these people get pulled away from their families to go here? Is it a new Colony? I've never heard of one up that way."

"It can't be new. It's too well developed. And a girl I talked to said it had been occupied before but there was a problem in the building. They abandoned it for a while."

"Who was this girl?"

I shrug, sitting back with my arms crossed over my chest. "Just some chick angry at being there."

"Another friend?" Ryan asks, grinning.

I shake my head. "I punched her in the face."

"Typical."

"And the ear. I almost knelt on her throat. Nearly smothered her with a pillow."

"Now do you see why I have a hard time believing you made friends in there?"

"This young woman," Crenshaw says suddenly, frowning at his map, "did she know if there were others? Other Colonies?"

"No, just the ones you have marked now."

He looks up at me, his face drawn. He's disappointed. "It is a shame you could not gain us more valuable information while you were there."

"It is. It's a shame I didn't do more sleuthing while I was there," I say, my temper rising. "I should have gone all Sherlock up in that joint, but I was too busy trying not to lose my mind from all of the bright lights and bodies everywhere. Next time, I promise, I'll do better."

Ryan isn't looking at me anymore. He's watching Crenshaw carefully, probably worried I'll upset him with my sarcasm. Part of me is worried too, but a bigger part is annoyed. Tired. Angry.

"What is this?" I demand, changing the subject.

I point to a dark area of the map, shaded in shadows with jagged strokes. It's in the south, just a few blocks from the two stadium Colonies sitting side by side.

"Hmmm," Crenshaw moans quietly. "That is a portal into Hell."

"Right."

"The space between here," he points to a narrow corridor running between the dark area and the Colonies, "is the Valley of the Shadow of Death. One must never, never pass through it."

"Of course not."

"But none of this is important, not right now. What I want to show you is this."

Crenshaw turns the map toward us. He points decisively to a small area at the very bottom. It's just the peak of a piece of land, nothing descript or defining about it at all. But written carefully over the top of it is the word *Elysium*.

"And what is that?"

Crenshaw smiles at me, his eyes wild. "Heaven."

"Oh, yeah," I say faintly, squinting at the map. "I can see it now."

"How is it Heaven, sir?" Ryan asks.

His foot nudges mine gently under the table. I don't know if it's on purpose, if it's a warning or an accident. Either way I don't like it and I move my feet away from him.

"It is an island in the south. It is completely and utterly wraith free."

"That's impossible."

"My boy, in Heaven nothing is impossible. This is where you will go to look for help."

"To where?" I ask feeling frustrated. "What is this? Who's there? I've never heard of anywhere being Risen free, nowhere real. It's all myth."

"It is a place like no other. One must only believe, to have faith in—"

"Crenshaw, what is it?" I snap, exasperated.

My patience for this conversation has died. I care about this guy, I really do, but I'm already pushed to my limits with everything else going on and now talking about the Colonies, being scolded for not getting better intel while I was in prison… I'm spent. I'm riddled with guilt and this ring pinching at my finger, growing tighter every single day, is dragging me down to the ground. I need answers. Real ones, not fairytales that will send me on adventures or journeys to strange mystical lands where I'm meant to ask for help from the fairies or the centaurs. If this is all the help he has, some slice of land in the south where he thinks he saw an angel once, then I have to get real and go to The Hive.

He looks at me in surprise, his eyes narrowing. "It is rude to interrupt, child. I thought you better than this."

"Well, I'm not. This has been fun, but I need the

real Crenshaw for a minute. Is he in there or am I wasting my time? Cause if he's not in, that's fine. I'll go get my help elsewhere."

He sits back in his seat, appraising me. "You mean the others."

"I mean The Hive."

"Joss," Ryan says quietly. His tone tells me that, yes, the foot nudge was a warning.

I ignore it and him.

"What's it going to be, Cren?"

There's a long tense silence in the small room. The smell of the onions is starting to give me a headache, the low light messing with my eyes and making them burn. As he continues to stare at me, something in his face changes. He's angry at me but there's something else too. Something I'm not equipped to read or understand.

"It is an island," Crenshaw finally says softly, "filled with people. Survivalists like myself. They cleared it of the wraiths, built homes, made it sustainable. They are very reclusive. Very exclusive. Many in my generation know of them but they are heavily guarded and not to be trifled with. You may join by invitation only and they stopped sending out invitations a long time ago."

"You had one, didn't you?" Ryan asks him gently.

Crenshaw nods sadly. "I did. I still do. I helped them years ago to set up their gardens for the apothecary. In exchange, I was given an open invitation to join them at any time."

"Why haven't you?" I ask.

He ignores me. He sits in silence staring down at the map. At the small point lovingly labeled *Elysium*.

"Why didn't you go?" Ryan finally asks.

"Because I would not leave her behind," he

whispers.

His daughter. Even I can follow this part of the conversation.

"Will they help us to take down the Colony? To overthrow A-36?" I ask.

He doesn't answer me directly. He doesn't look at me. "They despise the Colonies. They were once one of them. The original. Not on the island, but farther south in the deserts of another land. Of another time. A time when the war was waged with true armies and still we lost. Now our hope lies in you, in the two of you and… I am sorry. I have drifted off topic and you need answers. You need them *now*."

"Come on, Cren," I say, trying not to sound as annoyed as I feel. Or as guilty.

"If anyone will help you, it will be them."

"Do they have a name?" Ryan asks.

Crenshaw nods. "The Vashon. They took that name when they broke from the zealots. When innocent blood was shed and they would stand for it no longer, which is why they are your greatest hope. I learned my hatred of the zealots from them and trust me, it runs deep. If you go to the others they will betray you. They will steal from you, enslave you, murder you, but the very last thing they will ever do is help you. I hope you understand that." He stands abruptly. "Now if you'll excuse me, I've grown weary. I would be alone, thank you."

"Of course," Ryan agrees, standing quickly.

He puts his hand lightly on my back to usher me forward. I start to turn to snap at him but his touch turns impatient. I'm shoved out the door past Crenshaw before I can say a word. Ryan stays inside for a brief moment. Then he bows, accepts a light hand laid on the back of his head and that's it. Thus concludes the crazy portion of our day.

I turn silently to leave with Ryan, but when I look back at the small dark hut set deep in the woods, I feel sick in my stomach. Sad. We got information. We have a lead on a path to take around The Hive.

But I know I might have burned a bridge getting it.

Chapter Eight

Ryan and I walk in silence back to my loft. We have to deal with Risen along the way, but we take them down easily and without a word. We're surrounded at one point, something that should have scared me, should have sent my blood running cold through my veins and my heart hammering in my chest until it couldn't take it anymore and stopped. My breath should have died in my throat, a strangled moan escaping to be drowned out in the roar of moaning surrounding me. It should have happened because it's happened before.

But I was alone before.

This time Ryan and I immediately went back to back, my shorter body pressed up against his tall, broad one, and we faced off with the closing crowd. My missing arm is annoying but manageable. The pain is getting better meaning I'm getting better. Stronger. I'm healing and coming back from this thing that happened to me that left me broken. And, yes, I am well aware that it's only my bone that's healing. Whatever else was damaged is still fractured and jagged, cutting into everything and everyone around me.

When we get to my building, the second I step into the entryway, Ryan turns abruptly and begins to walk away. I stand amazed for a second, my jaw literally hanging slack as I watch him go.

"Where are you going?" I call after him.

He stops but he doesn't turn. "You're home. Now I'm going home."

"That's it? You're just going to leave without saying goodbye? Without say anything."

"Yeah."

"Why?"

He turns to look at me, his brow pulled tight in anger and amazement. "Are you serious? I'm pissed off, Joss."

"At me?"

"Oh my—" He throws his head back as he rubs the heels of his palms into his eyes. "Unbelievable."

"I know why you're mad," I say bitingly, getting annoyed that he's acting like this. I already feel guilty about so many things, I don't need this too. I don't need another lecture from another person telling me I'm doing it all wrong.

He drops his hands to stare at me. "Why? Why am I mad?"

"You think I don't know. That is so condescending! I'm not a child. I'm not an idiot."

"I think you don't understand. I *hope* you don't understand, because if you do then what you did back there was cruel and I really don't want to find out you're cruel. A lot of things I can overlook, but I will not deal with that."

"No one is asking you to deal with anything," I growl, taking several quick steps toward him. "No one asked you to 'overlook' anything. If there are things about me that you don't like, Ryan, then get the hell away from me. Leave me alone. You've been stalking me since the start. I didn't ask for this. I didn't ask for you or for them," I spit out, gesturing to the north, toward the Colony, "and I definitely didn't ask to be anyone's hero. So go ahead and go. Walk away and let me forget about you and the Colony and Crenshaw and Vin. It's all a mess anyway. I'll be better off without it."

Ryan closes the distance between us. He stops a single step away from me, staring down at me with his golden glowing eyes that make me want to cry. It's so humiliating. The tears are everywhere lately and if I'm not very careful, I could drown in them. I'll be like Alice from the Wonderland stories swimming in her own tears that refuse to stop because she's too scared and lost and alone.

"You can't do that. That's not how it works," Ryan tells me quietly, his anger seemingly gone. Poof, like magic. Like a burst balloon. "People aren't all or nothing. Friendships don't live and die on a single argument. You don't love everything about a person and you don't hate everything about them either. There are going to be things about you that I don't like, Joss, but not all of them will send me running. There are going to be things about me that you don't like—"

"So many," I mumble.

He grins faintly. "But you can't quit on me. Not until you find something you can't forgive. Cruelty I can't forgive. What about you?"

I swallow hard, shaking my head. I don't know what a deal breaker for me is. I've never had to think about it. All I know is that the only thing I will not abide from him is dying. But I can't say that because he won't promise me that it won't happen and I'll hate him for it. So instead, I make an effort at mending fences in the hope that someday soon I'll get good at it. And once I'm good at those, hopefully I'll feel strong enough to rebuild bridges.

"I wasn't being cruel," I tell him firmly. "At least I wasn't trying to be. I was impatient. I have this thing weighing on my chest, sitting like a sack of rocks on top of me and I can't shake it. Not until I get this done and it's already been weeks. I don't have time to sit around talking nonsense with him all day. *They* don't have time for that."

"Okay, that's fair. But remember, not all of his nonsense is nonsense."

"Ugh," I groan, dropping my head back. "I don't have time for riddles either."

"It's not a riddle. Look, you're smart. You'll figure it out. Why don't you go inside now? We've been out here awhile and we haven't been quiet. That's gotta be bugging you."

"Not as much as it should be," I mutter, looking up and down the street. It's empty. For now. "Are you still going home?"

He hesitates, watching me. "I probably should."

I grin. "Shoulda, woulda, coulda. What are you actually going to do?"

He kisses me. It's light and lingering. Surprising. His lips are the only part of him touching me and they're barely doing that. I feel exposed, open to the cold air while his heat is hovering nearby. It's amazing, breathless and free, like I want to be kissed like this by him for the rest of my life. I know he's done it on purpose. That he's keeping his distant, giving me space. That he's adapting to my own crazy, setting his watch to my cuckoo clock and it's incredible how that makes me feel. How it changes the kiss into more than skin against skin. It makes it a promise. An understanding. It doesn't feel closed in, doesn't feel confining. It feels light as air, heavy as sunshine.

He breathes warm across my mouth, making me shiver and smile. When he pulls away, he puts two steps between us.

"Now I know I should go home," he says, his voice deep.

I lift a skeptical eyebrow. "But are you going to?"

"I don't know."

"Come watch a movie with me," I blurt out. "We can watch *Pretty in Pink*."

"Why that one?" he asks, already closing the space between us again.

He's so easy.

"Because I don't like it."

"Then why would we watch it?" he laughs.

The sound of his voice echoing up and down the deserted street makes me smile. I should be cringing. I should be telling him to shush it or he'll get us killed. But I like the sound of his laughter all around me, the way it is in the loft when I feel the space shrink around him, becoming warmer. Brighter. Somehow more mine by his being there.

"You've seen what I like. Why wouldn't I show you what I don't like?"

He grins down at me, his eyes happy and full. "That's a really good point."

"Is that what people do?"

"I don't know. But it's what we do. When do I get to show you what I don't like?"

I roll my eyes, turning my back on him to head toward the building. "I already know what you don't like."

"Really? Hit me with it."

"You don't like when I'm mean. When I'm too

harsh."

"True, but I just told you that."

"You don't like it when I pull away from you."

He's silent behind me, no sound other than his footfalls in time with mine.

"You don't like it when you think I don't trust you," I continue.

"No, I don't like it when you absolutely, positively do not trust me."

I stop two steps up from him on the stairs, turning to look down at him.

"I do trust you. Probably more than I trust myself sometimes and that's scary. I don't like it, but I'm working on it. You've gotta give me time. It took me six years to be this way, it will take more than six weeks to change me."

"I don't want to change you, Joss."

I grin at his lie. "Yes, you do. At least a little." I shrug, continuing up the stairs. "And maybe it's not the worst thing in the world. Maybe it will do me good to let my guard down a little."

Famous last friggin' words.

When we open the door to my loft, I nearly scream. That's where I'm at on the threat level. Screaming. Let me make something crystal clear here; I. Do. Not. Scream. Ever. Not when they ate my parents, not when I ran into the street to find a world gone crazy, not even when they pounded on the outside of the car all day and all night as I lay shivering on the floorboards soaked in urine, sweat and fear. I never made a sound.

But now, finding Trent parked in the darkness in the middle of my loft, his eerie eyes fixed on my face like a hungry lion, I choke on a shriek.

"I will freakin' kill you," I breathe, begging my

heart to stop pounding in my chest. It aches from the pressure.

"Good to see you too," he drones.

"Come on, Trent, a little warning. We could have killed you, man," Ryan complains behind me.

Trent smirks. "Not on your best day."

"What do you want, psycho?" I demand.

"It's not what I want. It's what The Hive wants."

Ryan curses behind me. I second that. Trent just nods.

"They want to see me," Ryan eventually mumbles.

"They want to know why you're fighting again. And who it is you're fighting for."

"When?"

"Hours ago would have been best."

I glare at him. "You obviously knew we were downstairs. Why didn't you come tell us this? It's kind of important."

"And interrupt your magic moment? There are so few joys in this world anymore, why would I steal that from you two?"

I look at Ryan. "Is he messing with me or is he being serious? I can't read him."

"No one can," Ryan says. "He's written in backwards brail."

I glare at Trent again. "It'd be easier just to kill him."

"You're welcome to try."

Trent smiles.

"Alright, let's not waste time." I turn to Ryan, holding up my arm. "Take the splint off. Let's go."

He stares down at me for a long time, just looking. I wait patiently, my arm still held out to him.

"Would it to any good at all," he asks quietly, his

eyes imploring, "to ask you to stay here. Not tell you, but ask you nicely to stay here and wait for me?"

I take a deep breath, reminding myself I'm mending fences here. "I appreciate that you're not trying to tell me what to do. Consider your effort acknowledged."

"I'm marking it in the minutes of this conversation," Trent tells us.

"Not helping," Ryan mutters, glaring at him over my shoulder.

"But," I say firmly, shaking my arm to get Ryan's attention, "it doesn't change the fact that I'm coming with you. I'm the one with Vin's ring—"

"You could give it to me."

"And I'm the one who was sent in his place."

"They don't know that."

"I'm the one who knows about the Colony."

"You've told me what you know."

"I'm the one who was kidnapped, held prisoner, watched her friend nearly killed and murdered a woman in cold blood to get out!" I shout, deciding fences are overrated anyway. "I'm going!"

"Alright," Ryan says softly. Too softly. He steps closer, pushing my arm down out of the way. "Then what about this? They didn't ask to see you. They want to see me about the Underground. It has nothing to do with you and I can tell them that at the door if you try to go with me. You'll be locked out, treated like a girl from the stables."

"You wouldn't," I growl, fully believing the look in his eyes that says yes, he would.

He nods slowly. "Oh yeah, I would. If it means keeping you from going there, I would."

"I promised them, Ryan."

"And we'll keep your promise. I'll help you. We'll

go to the Vashons. We don't need The Hive."

"What's a Vashon?" Trent asks.

I bristle, hating the interruption, but I bite my tongue because I've already shouted at one of them in the last few minutes. I'm not looking to lash out at everyone. Not yet.

"A group Crenshaw mentioned. We were just with him asking his advice," Ryan tells him, still standing in my space.

He's towering over me, probably to intimidate me, but what he doesn't know (what I'll never tell him) is that it's comforting. Eye level with his chest, seeing his shoulders go on for miles, knowing the strength lying in wait inside; it's comforting. He has my back and he's strong enough to rely on. I can let a little bit of the weight of the world pass on to him and he can take it. That's terrifyingly wonderful. It's why I don't step away. Not because I don't want to retreat. Don't want to show weakness. Okay, that's part of it, but mostly it's because I just like it. I like him.

"They live on an island down south. It's supposed to be Risen free," I tell Trent.

"That's a sweet fairytale," Trent chuckles.

"I don't think it is. I think it's for real. At least it was the last he knew of it. Either way, it's worth a try. It's a better option than owing anything to The Hive."

"But what if it's not real?" I ask, looking up into his face. "What if we get there and it's nothing? Then we need The Hive anyway and we lost our shot at talking to them."

Ryan shakes his head, his eyes locked on mine. "I'd rather take the risk that they don't exist than risk taking you—"

"We'd need a boat."

Ryan and I both turn to look at Trent.

"Why?"

"It's an island, right? We'd need a boat to get to it. Do you have a boat?"

I shake my head even though I imagine I'm not meant to answer that question.

"No," Ryan admits darkly.

"Well then, problem solved," Trent says happily, standing. "We need The Hive after all."

Chapter Nine

Ryan, Trent and I walk through the dark streets together, heading for The Hive. This area is relatively cleared of Risen, not much of a surprise. But the empty, silent streets make me more nervous than a horde would. It's ominous and horrifying. I'm shaking a little, though I'd never let them know it. My arm is aching being out of the splint, the thin material of my worn, black fleece the only protection it has left. It's not ready. Maybe I'm not ready. But the dull yellow glow of the lights inside the aquarium are burning at the end of the street and it's too late to turn back now.

"Crenshaw isn't going to be happy about this," Ryan grumbles.

"Cren ain't gots to know 'bout it."

He looks over at me, his face worried and confused. "Are you alright?"

"No," I mutter, wiping my sweating palms on my pants. "I'm freaking out a little."

"It shows. What was that?"

"I've heard the gangs talk like that before," I say defensively.

"Well, most don't so, you know… don't."

"Thanks for the advice."

He glances over at me, the confusion gone but the

worry etched deep in his eyes. "I won't let them keep you here."

"That's not what I'm worried about."

I won't let them keep me here.

"Then what are you afraid of?" Trent asks.

"Did I say I was afraid? No one said afraid. Let's keep it on the real, boys."

"Stop that," Ryan reminds me.

"Right, yeah. I'm not afraid. I'm just freaked. It's different."

"What are you freaked about?"

"There are Risen in there. In a crowded room. That's a big red flag right there; the mass of people. I'm not a fan."

"Joss, you know it takes a long time to turn. Way longer than it used to."

"But there are tons of people in there that come in contact with Risen for fun. I'm not done worrying you'll still turn from being around them with your open cuts. What kind of wounds do all of them have? How old are they?"

"We cleaned mine early, I'm fine. Calm down. It's not like it used to be."

"If a person is bitten, though—"

"They're done for, I know. But we'll be out of there way before they turn."

"It's stupid."

"Keep that to yourself when you get in there."

"I'm not great at censoring myself."

"Maybe don't talk at all," Trent suggests.

Ryan and I both glare at him. He shrugs, unconcerned.

"You can talk, just be careful what you say," Ryan tells me. "Less is more."

"I tried to say that about her clothes and you told me to f—"

"Don't start that again," Ryan warns Trent.

"What about my clothes?" I ask, glancing down at my tattered jeans and too large coat.

Trent smirks at me. "You look like a tomboy."

"Because I am, Trent."

"I told him we should bring you in looking like a stable girl. It would make more sense."

"And I said drop it," Ryan warns him, his voice becoming hot.

"Like a pro?" I ask, shocked.

But then I wonder why I'm shocked. How else are they meant to explain me? Where have I been hiding if not inside a stable? I'll cause more of a stir walking in looking like this, like I don't owe anyone anything, than I would waltzing in naked. I'm definitely not doing that, that's insane and I'm pretty sure it's so far outside my comfort zone that I'd vomit from the stress, but it's something to consider.

I quickly strip off my jacket, carefully peeling it over my aching arm.

"Hold this," I snap at Trent, throwing the jacket in his face.

It falls away to reveal his feline smile, his eyes watching me in the dark.

"Joss, you don't have to change how you look," Ryan says, sounding tired.

"Yes, I do," I tell him, pulling my t-shirt up over my head.

I don't have anything on underneath but a thin tank top and a sports bra, but it'll have to do. My education on sexy comes from 80's movies but I somehow doubt fluffing my hair and wearing neon spandex is what I need to blend in these days.

"You need to eat more," Trent says, pointing at my side. "I can see your ribs."

I snatch my coat back from him, wincing as pain shoots up my arm.

"If I had more to eat, I'd eat it. Back off me."

"You're not taking good care of your girl, Ry."

"I would if she'd let me," Ryan mutters.

He's staring down at me as well. Mostly at my chest.

"Alright," I growl at both of them, "eyes forward and hands off. Let's go get this over with."

We move under an overpass, crumbling and decrepit. I hurry as I always do going under them, worried that they'll choose that moment to dissolve down on top of me. To trap me as easy pickings for... well, just about anyone, living or undead. I shiver at the thought of all the enemies I have out there, a fair portion of which are in this building looming in front of me. It's stupid to be here.

The building is two stories of good condition that screams someone lives there. The exterior paint is badly chipped and faded, but broken windows are carefully boarded up and the surrounding areas are barricaded and secured. It's a long building stretching out onto a pier over the water of the Pudget Sound. I've fished there before. Not by this building, obviously, but hidden farther north away from The Hive and the Colonies nearby. I can see them now. The stadiums are just south of us, also glowing faintly in the night sky. All of them so shamelessly broadcasting where they are and what they have. Hardly a care in the world.

I hate all of them.

The inside of the building is dark as far as I can see,

but Ryan doesn't hesitate to walk right up to the door and knock sharply. It doesn't take long for a small square in the door to pop open.

"What?" a voice asks gruffly.

Ryan puts his face to the hole. "I'm here to see the Boss. He asked for me."

"You're not here to fight?"

"No. Just business."

"That's a shame. Slow night."

"Not my problem," Ryan says, his tone dead.

I hear a muffled chuckle as the square slams shut. Bolts are unlatched and eventually the door swings open. There are lights on inside but not much. The entire entryway is cast in black shadows, including the bouncer at the door, and I hesitate as all of my survival instincts scream at me to run the other way. Nature and numbers. They don't lie.

Ryan steps inside, not bothering to look back to see if Trent and I are following him. Trent nudges me subtly with his arm, falling in step behind me as I stumble forward. I keep moving, my muscles jerky with the tremors running through them. I probably look like one of the junkies. Someone itching for a fix. Better to look like an addict than a coward.

We come into a large open area with high ceilings and exposed beams. The remnants of a huge fish tank sits on the opposite side of the room. It's emptied of water but looks like it's filled with something else. Shoes maybe? It's too dark to tell and I'm too freaked to wander over and look. I hang close to Trent, of all people.

I am knee deep in Neverland now. There are so, so, so many Lost Boys. They're milling around the lobby, swarming everywhere. No one close, but they're on the peripheral. Walking on the catwalks above us, sitting around what was once a reception desk to the left and a lot of them are coming and going behind the fish tank. Back there must either be where the fights or the girls are.

The people, they don't bother me so much. I got pretty used to it at the Colony, though I never learned to like it. What's bugging me more than anything is the darkness and the lights. It's too dark to see well, to know who is who and what their life status is. But the light annoys me more. Strung all over the building are strands of LED Christmas lights of every color. I hate Christmas lights. Christmas trees, Christmas music, Christmas presents, but I absolutely cannot stand Christmas lights. These LEDs make the movements of the people around me seem strange, almost like a strobe light. I try my hardest to ignore them but it's like ignoring the sun. It's everywhere.

"Ryan," a high pitched voice sings out.

We all turn to see a girl about my age walking down the stairs from the catwalks. She's wearing next to nothing. Tiny little shorts and a tinier tank top. Her long blond hair looks pretty clean, making me wonder if The Hive has hot showers. I'm pretty sure they don't get their soap from Crenshaw.

"Elise," he says, his voice no warmer than it was for the bouncer.

"I thought that was you. I missed you the last couple times you were here."

"I wasn't here to socialize."

"What about tonight?" she purrs, walking right up to him and pressing her hand against his stomach. "Do you have time to be social tonight?"

I go to take a step toward them, but Trent stealthily

grabs my hand. Thank goodness it's my good hand, because he crushes it in his. When I glare up at him, trying to pull it out of his grasp, he shakes his head minutely. I freeze, waiting.

Ryan steps back from the girl. She steps forward, regaining the ground and giggling up at him.

"Not a good time, El. I'm here to see the Boss tonight."

"What about after? You might want a midnight snack."

He jerks his head toward Trent and I. "I packed a lunch."

I want to punch him, but I remind myself that being a trick was my idea.

Elise smiles happily. "Ryan, finally taking a taste! It's about time." She glances over at me, frowning. "She's scrawny, though. Where'd she come from?"

"I don't know. She's on loan from the Pikes."

The girl scrunches her nose in disgust at me. "Geez, Ryan, are you that hard up? There are girls here that would give it up to you for free and you wouldn't have to check them for fleas."

"Just crabs," I say sharply.

"What did you say?" she shrieks.

"I said you're a dock walker," I enunciate slowly. Loudly. "No doubt you're crawling with crabs."

"You're dead," she breathes, taking several steps toward me.

I'm itching for her to come closer. Just a little bit closer. Even with Trent destroying my good hand and my other arm on the mend, I could beat this chick into the ground. She won't remember her own name when I'm done with her.

"You're just mad because she's right, Elise," a

voice flows down from the rafters, a soft southern drawl making her bitter words sound sweet.

We all look up to see a woman with long dark hair making her way toward the stairs. She's beautifully pale and dressed almost the same way I am, only her bra, if she had one on, would be working a lot harder than mine.

"Now get away from Ry before I remove you myself."

Elise backs away, glaring.

The dark haired woman stops at the bottom of the stairs, staring expectantly at Elise.

"Disappear."

I'm disappointed when she does.

"Thanks, Freedom," Ryan says, walking up to the woman to give her a hug.

It doesn't bother me the way Elise's hands on him did. My veins don't run hot, my hands itching for a fight. For a knife.

"No problem," Freedom tells him warmly. "Your brother would never want to see you around a girl like Elise and neither do I. But what are you doing here? You're not fighting tonight are you?"

"No, I got called in to see the Boss."

Freedom looks at him long and hard. "That's never good."

Ryan shrugs. It looks stiff. "I think he just wants to talk about the fights I was in recently. I'm not signing on with him. Don't worry."

"Anytime anyone goes in to see the Boss, I always worry. Be careful, alright?"

"Yeah."

"Freedom!"

She closes her eyes briefly. I imagine her counting

to ten in her head. When she opens them, she turns to face a tall, shirtless bald guy stalking toward her.

"What do you want, Dante?"

"Are you seriously giving me attitude right now? You're supposed to be in the Arena at the table full of Westies. The other girls are already there but they're asking for *you*."

Freedom rolls her eyes at this hulking man covered in tats, towering at least six inches over her. "Why are you even doing business with them? I told you, they're idiots."

"Idiots with deep pockets. Get in there."

"I'll be there in a minute."

"Freedom, I'm not dealing with you tonight. Get in there now."

I hold my breath as I watch his hands, worried he'll hit her soon. I've seen women treated worse than that and this one is pushing the limits. Inside, I'm begging her to just go.

"Dante," she says quietly, her accent becoming more pronounced. Less sweet. "If you tell me to get in there one more time, I will cut you. Do you understand me? I will cut you so deep your grandma in the grave will feel it. Now, I said I'll be there in a minute and I meant it."

Dante shakes his head, a harsh breath coming out his nose, but I see his mouth twitch at the corners. "One minute."

"Isn't that what I said?"

"You're insane."

"Get out of here."

He turns to leave, shouting over his shoulder, "Fifty seconds!"

"Unbelievable," Freedom mutters. She turns to

Ryan. "You better get to that meeting. You know where to go?"

"Yeah, unfortunately."

She pats him affectionately on the shoulder as she steps past him. "You need anything, you come find me, alright?"

"Thanks, Freedom."

"Thirty seconds!"

"Oh, Grandma Jean is gonna be in a world of hurt, I swear to you!" Freedom shouts as she saunters off in the direction Dante is disappearing.

Ryan looks at me, his face tense. "You could wait out here. Trent could stay with you."

"You shouldn't go in there alone," Trent tells him.

"She can't stay out here alone."

"So she won't stay out here at all," I snap.

I'm grateful for the rage I felt toward Elise. The excitement at the idea of dismantling her has chased the shakes away. I don't feel any braver, but I'm not outwardly pissing myself in fear either. Progress.

"We do this together or we don't do it at all," I say, my voice a little softer.

Ryan sighs, but he nods reluctantly. Trent and I follow him toward the reception desk where we cut right down a dark hallway. Another bouncer with dark almond eyes and perfect mocha skin stops us, gives Ryan the runaround about fighting just like everyone else, then finally leads us to a closed white door. I'm surprised that he doesn't knock. Just opens it up and sends us right in.

The office isn't much, but it is large. There are small square tables arranged in every corner, all of them occupied by a few people speaking in hushed voices, but at the far end of the room there's a large half circle of couches arranged on a platform. There are several men of all ages seated on the couches, all of them talking loudly and laughing. Not too loudly to miss our entrance, though.

"Ryan!" a tall man with long, shaggy hair graying around the temples exclaims. He sits forward in his seat, his eyes landing on Ryan and looking excited. I don't like that look.

Ryan nods slightly. "Marlow."

So this is Captain Hook in the flesh.

"Good of you to join us. I sent for you hours ago."

"I came when I got the message."

Marlow leans to the side dramatically, eyeing Trent with mock suspicion. "Maybe I sent the wrong messenger."

"No, I was... unreachable for a while." Ryan gestures over his shoulder to me.

I can feel every eye at the circle of couches fall on me. I'm acutely aware of the clothes I'm wearing but I'm more aware of what I'm not wearing. I long for the jacket draped over my arm but to put it on now would be to hide. To show weakness. So I square my shoulders, raise my chin, and even though the shakes are coming back, I keep my eyes locked on Marlow's.

"Now that," he says softly, eyeing me, "I can most certainly forgive. Where did she come from?"

Ryan shrugs, casually scanning the room. "I don't know. She's a loaner from the Elevens."

I thought I was from the Pikes, I think.

I nearly scowl, nearly pinch my brow in confusion, but I lock it down. Marlow is still watching me closely.

He grins, sitting back in his seat. Finally his eyes fall to Ryan again and I can breathe.

"I'll have to get in touch with them. They have

better inventory than I thought. But I'm glad you're finally here. You and I need to talk. It's come to my attention that you've come out of retirement."

"You've been lied to. I'm not fighting for anyone."

Marlow's eyes go round in surprise. "Really? I saw you fight with my own eyes."

Ryan shakes his head. "I was dealing with Kevin's death. I needed an outlet. I worked it out in the ring. I'm over it now."

"Just like that, eh?"

"It wasn't so easy."

"No, I doubt it was. So you're not fighting under the Hyperions?"

"No. I'm not fighting for anyone."

"Not even for the right price?"

"I'm not as good as he was. I'll die sooner rather than later."

Marlow nods slowly, his eyes drifting around the room. "You're right about that. You're not as good as your brother was, but you're still one of the best out there. And I do hate to see talent go to waste." His eyes land on me again. "A sure fire money maker is so hard to find."

"I'm not in the market," Ryan tells him firmly.

"A shame. Well, then be on your way, I guess. If we have nothing else to say to each other."

Ryan nods again, then starts to back out of the room. His hand grips mine gently, careful of my injured arm. I go willingly when he pulls on it.

"Hold on," Marlow calls. "Leave the girl. I'll return her to the Elevens."

Ryan freezes, his grip tightening painfully. "I can't. She's checked out in my name."

Marlow waves his hand. "I'll return her for you. I'll

even pay your fee on top of my own. I'd like a taste of what they've got up there."

Ryan is breathing fast and hard, his grip not loosening.

Marlow's eyes shift to Ryan slowly. "Is there a problem?"

"She's not staying."

Marlow smiles. "Either she's staying or we have a problem. Do you want to have a problem with me, Ryan?"

"She knows Vin," Trent speaks up calmly. All eyes dart to him. "She has a message from him."

Marlow doesn't miss a beat, though his smile disappears. "Vin is no longer with us."

"Not with you here, but he is alive."

That's a big maybe, I think, but I keep it to myself.

Trent looks at me with his intense eyes. They speak volumes, all of them saying *don't mess this up.*

"Show him the ring."

I look at Ryan meaningfully. He releases my hand but his eyes are tight, full of worry and regret. I smile faintly at him before I turn to Marlow, hoping it's reassuring. I raise my hand, showing Marlow the large ring on my finger.

He eyes it without emotion, his face completely placid. I can't tell if he actually recognizes it. Then he speaks and the entire room freezes from the chill of his tone. I know immediately I've struck a chord with the ring but the tension rolling through the room makes me worry it's one I shouldn't have hit. It makes me wonder if I'm making it out of this room with all my fingers.

"Out," he says coldly, his eyes hard on mine. "Everyone out. *Now.*"

Chapter Ten

"When did you steal that ring from him?" Marlow asks, his voice so low I barely hear it.

My heart is in my throat. I have to swallow to speak, but I hold his eye because I know to look away is to admit something. Guilt, lies, theft, murder. None of these will get us out of this room unscathed. It's emptied out except for the three of us, Marlow and a few men scattered around the room guarding all the exits. Guarding the Boss.

"He gave it to me."

"Bullshit."

"It's not. I was in the Colony with him. I was in the van with him when he, Nats and Breanne were taken."

Marlow watches me closely, debating. The fact that I know the girls' names might give me some credibility. Or I might just be a pro with good listening skills on market day.

"You were in a Colony with him."

It's not a question. It's a dubious statement. Like saying 'So, you're the tooth fairy'.

"Yes."

"But you're standing here now."

"Yes."

"Try again. How'd you get that ring?"

"He gave it to me," I insist firmly, sticking to my story. "He told me to bring it to you. That you'd recognize it because he said it was his old man's and it's the only thing that's ever meant anything to him."

I'm spinning the ring nervously on my finger the way Vin did when he was thinking. I stop when I notice Marlow watching me do it.

"Why would he give it to you to bring to me?"

I breathe deeply.

Here we go.

"Because the people in the Colony, they want to make a deal. They want your help. Vin was supposed to be the one standing here telling you all of this. The Colonists were going to break him out with the promise that he'd come back with help."

"What do Colonists need help with?" he snarls.

"Getting out. Not all of them are happy. They're trapped just like I was. Just like Vin is. Slaves in their own home. They want to overthrow the leaders, take control of the building and get their freedoms back."

"And Vin promised to help with this?"

"He said he'd try," I reply weakly.

Marlow chuckles, shaking his head. "Now I know you're lying. You never knew Vin. You may have met him, you certainly robbed him, which is impressive in and of itself, but if you knew him you'd know you're talking crazy. That man wouldn't lift a finger to save his own mother even if it wouldn't cost him anything. He's not what you call altruistic."

I shake my head, feeling foolish.

"It means selfless," Trent says quietly behind me.

My face burns with embarrassment, my temper flaring.

"He wasn't going to come back to help us," I say

sharply to Marlow. "He was going to betray us all. He knew it, Nats knew it, I knew it. You seem to know it. But he messed up. He started sleeping with a crazy bitch who stabbed him, maybe killed him."

Marlow blinks. "See, now *that* I believe."

"Wouldn't be the first time," the bouncer who brought us in mutters.

"I was there when it happened. I was with him. She came at me and… and I killed her. Vin was injured, he couldn't go and I had just killed one of their leaders so I couldn't stay. We traded places. He gave me this ring, told me to come to you, told me that it would never work and then I left him there on the ground, bleeding." My throat is closing again but it's not from anxiety or fear. It's from wondering. Worrying. Caring. "I didn't leave him alone. One of the rebels from inside took the keys from the dead woman and got me out. He stayed with Vin. But I don't know if he survived. I—I hope he did."

"What do the Colonists want?" Marlow asks. He sounds genuinely curious but something else too. Distant somehow. Like he's asking about things that have no bearing on his life in any way. Like I'm telling him an entertaining story. "What deal was Vin bringing?"

"They want you to storm the Colony in the north."

"There is no Colony in the north."

"Yes, there is. It's in the old MOHAI building. The museum."

"That Colony went down mo—" someone begins.

"Shut up!" Marlow calls out at them, his eyes never leaving me. I struggle not to jump. He tells me softly, "Continue."

I take a calming breath. It doesn't help.

"The people will overthrow it from inside. It'll be

easy for you to take it down from the outside. They'll give it to you in return. They don't want it. All of them were brought there from other Colonies. From the stadiums and the south. They want to go home, they just need you to get them out. Then they'll let you have the MOHAI."

"Oh, they'll let me have it? And they'll just go home. Everyone will get what they want, no problem?" Marlow asks sarcastically.

"Yes," I say, but I know it's a lie.

"Here's how that plays out in the real world. I send men to help overthrow the MOHAI. It goes down easy, just as you said. We take it over, the Colonists leave. Brilliant. Perfect. But here's where it goes wrong. The people who leave, they go back to their homes. To the other Colonies. They show up, wanting to come in and suddenly the people running the big show are wondering what the hell happened to the MOHAI. So they come looking and find us there. Then they wipe us out. It's happened before. Do you think they were the only ones with the idea of taking the stadiums? They weren't! I will not risk a David and Goliath war over a pimp's promise that he would have broken the second he got out."

"David won," Trent says, seemingly oblivious to the rage written all over Marlow's face. To the wrath dripping from his tone.

I try not to flinch, but I fail.

Blood in the water.

"I tried," I say, trying to sound strong. To make up for my small mistake. "That's all I told them I'd do. I understand why you won't do it, but you have to understand why I had to try. We'll find the help we need somewhere else."

"Where do you think you'll find it? With the Hyperions?" Marlow asks bitingly. "They don't even know these two traitors are here. They don't know he's been fighting. I can have him kicked out tomorrow with what's happened here tonight. Where will you find help then?"

My heart aches in my chest. I hadn't thought of that. How had I not considered that? Ryan has betrayed his gang, Trent too. They'll be banished if they're found out. The gangs are insane about loyalty and the things they've been doing, the lying and fighting and the sneaking around, it's all been for nothing. For me. And it will cost them everything.

I want to turn to them, to apologize, but I can't. I can't leak more blood in this shark tank. I might not make it out alive as it is.

"The Vashons," I say, grasping at straws. "We're going to the island."

Marlow doesn't blink. He doesn't breathe. He only stares at me with his burning eyes and a frown etched on his face. It's been there since I brought up Vin and I recognize that symptom. Marlow has the same disease I do. He cares. He cares about Vin, about where he is and if he's alive. That's why he's so angry at me. He had written him off, buried his body in the Sound, then I walked in and resurrected him before his eyes.

I'll pay for that. For the hope. For that dirtiest of dirty words.

"The island, huh? That's... something. What is that, Rex?" Marlow asks over his shoulder. "What would you call that?"

"Stupid."

"Suicidal," someone else agrees.

"I think it's perfect," Marlow says happily. His

happy is freakier than his pissed off. I fight another flinch when he smiles at me. "I'll tell you what. If you get the Vashons to come up here and help you with your war, we'll back your play."

This feels dangerous. Everything in this place feels dangerous. Especially that smile.

"And if they won't help?"

He shrugs carelessly. "Then nothing. Then you're on your own. You don't bring this to me again."

"What's the catch?"

He chuckles. "Why do you assume there's a catch?"

I don't answer.

He grins knowingly. Appreciatively. "Let's just say I'll be impressed if you get the elitists off their island. So impressed that I'll be willing to help you in any way I can."

"Deal."

"Joss," Ryan murmurs. I can feel him move close beside me.

"We need a boat to reach the island," Trent tells Marlow.

I hear Ryan sigh. We've run away from him, sprinting down a hill full steam with no chance of stopping. Not until we're forced to. Or until we fall.

"You're full of needs and wants, aren't you?" Marlow asks. He nods as he rises, as he makes his way off the platform to stand in front of us. "You can borrow a boat. For a price."

I actually feel better talking cost with him. It's solid. It's real. It's not smoke and mirrors, smiles and scowls that pretend to mean one thing but really mean another entirely.

"What will it cost?" I ask.

"Dammit," Ryan mutters.

I glance at him, unsure. He's frowning at me.

"We should have had more Market 101 discussions. That's not a great way to negotiate."

"We can negotiate with him?" I whisper.

"Everything is negotiable, kid," Marlow tells me. "You just gotta make sure you know the worth of what you want. How much is getting this boat worth to you?"

I shake my head, completely at a loss. I don't have anything, definitely not anything they don't already have.

"Not flush at the moment, huh? That's alright. We can still do business. Tell me, what did Vin value you at?"

"What?" I ask, stunned and angry at where this conversation is going.

"The man's a professional. He can't help himself. No way he spent any amount of time with you and didn't slap a price tag on you. So, what was it?"

I open my mouth to answer, to lie and say he never told me, but Ryan cuts me off.

"I'll fight."

"No!" I snap at him.

He ignores me. He locks eyes with Marlow with a cold indifference.

"I'll do it. That should be worth a boat."

Marlow considers him for a long, painful moment.

"You'll fight for me?"

"No, just one fight. Tonight. That's it."

"How does that benefit me? Everyone bets on you. I'd make pennies off it."

"Not if I fight in the Blind."

Marlow grins. "Really?"

"Once. I'll do it one time."

"That's as often as anyone ever does it."

"What's the Blind?" I ask.

Again, I'm ignored. I'm reminded of Crenshaw and Ryan in the hut and I worry this is becoming a thing.

"You'd be the only one to know," Ryan tells him. "The only person betting high on the Blind."

"Won't that create some suspicion?"

Ryan shrugs, scowling at Marlow. "It's your club isn't it? What do you care what they think? Bet under a different name. Send a lackey down to do it."

"Hmmm." Marlow turns, his head hanging forward as he thinks. Finally he turns to face us again, his hand stretched out to Ryan. "You have yourself a deal."

Ryan shakes firmly with him, his face going blank. The guilt I carry like a stone in my stomach grows until it feels like it will break me in two. I hate all of this, myself included.

"You'll have a boat on loan. As soon as the fight is done I'll have the boys bring it around."

"Bring it around now," Ryan says, his voice low. Quiet.

Marlow raises a surprised eyebrow at him. "And why would I do that?"

"We agreed you'd lend us a boat if I fight. I'll fight, I gave my word. But win or lose, these two get the boat. So I'll go to the Arena from here and you'll have the boat brought around."

"Win or lose, as in live or die?" I ask him. Sick of being ignored, I get into his space, forcing him to look at me.

He glances down at me. His normally warm eyes are hard. Empty.

"Yes."

"I suppose you're right," Marlow agrees. I can feel

his eyes on me. I can feel him thinking. "Just as a point of curiosity, what *did* Vin price you as?"

I shouldn't tell him. I should shut up. I should lock it down. I should lie and tell him I'm a dime. Nothing better than blank-faced Breanne. But I'm pissed. I'm mad that Ryan is going into a fight for my sake. I'm mad that I've been put into this position, that I've been forced out of hiding and thrust into this world of killers and douchebags. That I'm ruining Ryan and I'm passively watching it happen. So I do something stupid. Something emotional.

"He called me a Benjamin," I tell him fiercely, looking him hard in the eyes.

He grins, his face openly surprised. "Really? Wow." He looks me up and down, appraising me in new light. I can feel Ryan's eyes on me too. I don't know what they hold. I can only handle the weight of Marlow's stare at the moment. "Well, he is the professional. I never would have seen it but… he would know, I suppose. Interesting."

No one asks him why it's interesting. I have a feeling everyone else already knows.

"Rex," Marlow calls out, still looking at me with a luminous grin. "Get the maps. They'll need to take a look at them before they go. We wouldn't want them getting lost. Not with my boat."

Rex brings in a large roll that he spreads out on a table. It's an old map of the Sound and Seattle from back when streets had names and places had purpose beyond shelter from the storm. It looks nothing like Crenshaw's and I miss the naked mermaid happily telling me hello. This map feels cold in comparison.

"We have so many maps here. Of the entire world, what's left of it," Marlow muses, pouring over the paper. "Every corner mapped out, every story told. It's a shame really. No matter how exotic a locale, it's made almost boring. Mundane." He looks up at me with that creepy grin again. "There are so few uncharted territories left. So few untouched lands. They're a gem when you can find them."

I stare at him blankly, silently. I don't want to encourage this conversation any further. Partly because I don't understand it, but also because I think I'm beginning to.

Chapter Eleven

Ryan is led away by two of the guards, ushered out flanked on each side by them as though he were a flight risk. I watch him go, my stomach dropping out, my heart pinching in my chest. He doesn't look back and I haven't decided yet if that makes it better or worse.

Trent and I are given the rundown with the maps. We're instructed on where exactly the Vashon's island is and the best way to get there. Apparently everyone and their mother knows where this thing is but no one attacks it. No one bothers them. That's very telling right there. Like this aquarium and the stadiums. Who are these people? What are we getting ourselves into by going to them? By going somewhere The Hive doesn't dare to go.

I let Trent examine the maps, his crazy eyes absorbing every detail and committing it all to memory. I'm too distracted to deal with it. I keep thinking about Ryan, about where they've taken him, about what exactly this Blind business is. I really hope it's not what it sounds like.

Finally, Trent and I are released. That's it, just shoved out the door. Thanks for stopping by, get the hell out. They tell us the boat will be waiting at the end of the pier and we're welcome to take it at any time. I'm relieved when Trent leads me through the entryway toward the shoe filled fish tank. I was worried he'd take me out of here, that Ryan told him not to let me see him fight. It would have killed me and I would have fought him tooth and nail to stay. No part of me believes that I could win in a fight with Trent, though. Even if I was fully healed and armed, he'd lay me on my ass.

He silently takes me back behind the tank, down another long, dark hallway, down a cramped flight of stairs lit with emergency red lights and straight into the freak show.

The Arena is my worst nightmares made real.

It's a large dark room full of makeshift risers that creak and groan as people walk on them. They form a circle around a dome in the middle made of concrete with squares punched out to see inside. And what's inside is what's horrifying. Risen. Several Risen tethered to benches around the outside rim of the dome.

"It used to be a huge fish tank," Trent tells me. He has to pull me gently along because my feet have frozen to the floor. I do not want to enter this room. "The part we're in, the *outside*, is actually the tank. There used to be glass in those squares between the concrete so people inside the dome could look out at the fish."

"Now we're doing the opposite," I mutter, staring at the Risen that shuffle and groan down on the main floor.

"No," Trent says darkly. "Now we're just fools dancing with Death, begging to die."

I look up at him in surprise. I've never heard his feathers ruffled before, but he's angry. He hates this. But he's done it before.

"Why did you do it if—"

"Is it true?" Freedom asks me, coming out of

nowhere and scaring the crap out of me.

"Whoa," I say, convincing myself not to hit her when she rolls up on me, getting in close.

"Is it true?" she insists in a sharp whisper.

"Is what true?"

"About Vin. Is he alive?"

Word gets around fast in the shark tanks.

"Yeah," I tell her, trying to back up. "Last I saw."

She swears on a sigh. "I knew he was too evil to die."

Before I can react to that, before I can wrap my head around the insult that sounds like a sweet compliment on her southern tongue, she's gone. Trent pulls me to the top of the risers, though I wish he wouldn't. I don't trust these things. They're shaking side to side every time someone new comes to stand on them. It's like the overpass – I can just see it giving way, crushing us all. I can see the Risen getting loose. Attacking the crowd. The low lights reflecting the blood as it sprays over every surface. The screams echoing, pulsing with panic as people scramble over each other. The bites. The growling. The sickly slurps. My mother's eyes.

"Joss," Trent says impatiently, bumping me with his shoulder. "What's the matter with you?"

"Nothing," I snap, blinking rapidly. Asking my eyes to swallow back the moisture brimming around them. "What happens now?"

He leans in close to speak in my ear. I tense from my toes to my tonsils.

"Because there's a volunteer for the Blind," he murmurs low and deep, "that'll be the main event. The only event for the night. That's what everyone is betting on right now. They don't know who has volunteered, it's kept secret, but they're betting on whether or not he'll survive."

"Is it barehanded?" I ask, not understanding the huge risk, aside from the obvious. I've seen Ryan fight off a Risen. I've seen him fight off a lot of Risen. He's unstoppable. This doesn't sound like the lost cause I worried it would be.

Trent nods his head solemnly. "And blindfolded."

"What?!" I shriek.

He looks at me pointedly. Doesn't say anything, just stares at me.

"Why?" I whisper.

"It makes it a challenge."

"It's suicide. Has he ever done this before?"

"No," Trent says, looking away. But not fast enough. He's worried.

And now I'm over here growing ulcers on top of my ulcers.

"If he runs into trouble," I ask, my voice breathy and frail, "what will happen if I run in there and help him?"

"They'll kill you both on the spot. They don't abide cheating here."

"They're cheating now," I hiss indignantly.

Trent shrugs.

"This is crap," I grumble.

"This is The Hive."

By the time some idiot in a sleeveless muscle T saunters into the center of the Arena, my leg is twitching like I'm having a seizure. Trent looks at me, at my leg, then back at me again. I stare at him, begging him to say something. To give me a reason. He smirks and looks away.

"Welcome to the Arena!" muscle man shouts.

He spins in a circle to address the entire crowd. They go insane. My eyes dart around nervously as people shoot to their feet, cheering and shouting. They're a bloodthirsty bunch.

"In this Blind," I ask Trent, leaning in to shout in his ear over the din of the crowd, "are the Risen blinded too?"

He frowns at me. "That wouldn't be very sporting."

"Are you freakin' kidding me right now?"

"I rarely kid. Pay attention, Joss. Your boy is about to make his entrance."

I'm on my feet before I even think about it. I have to stand to see over the crowd in front of me pressing in on the dome. People have climbed the cement exterior to look down inside from the top. I'm sure it's a great view but one false move and you're inside the Arena. I doubt they pause the games to safely remove the fallen.

"We have a treat tonight!" muscle man cries. "As you know, we have a volunteer for the Blind!"

The crowd loses its mind again. The noise is deafening and I wonder how I've never heard it before, even all the way across town in my loft. They quiet down instantly as the announcer raises his hand, calling for order.

"You've placed your bets. You've weighed the odds. You've seen the Risen that will fight tonight. But you don't know who your champion will be. Are you excited to find out?"

"Yes!!!" the crowd cries in unison.

"Did you vote for them to live?"

"Booo!!!" is the nearly unanimous reply.

The announcer grins maliciously. "Some of you are going to go home angry tonight. I give you your champion in the Blind…. Ryan Hyperion!!!"

There are moans, more boos, curses and exclamations of outrage. Ryan steps out into the middle of the ring wearing nothing but a pair of ratty cut off shorts. His skin is everywhere, open to the air, to our eyes. To their hands. To their mouths. It makes me feel dizzy with how wrong it is. How dangerous. But the crowd is still hissing at him, some people throwing things inside the Arena in their rage. The crowd, in a word, is angry.

"What's happening? Do they hate him?"

"No," Trent says with a smug smile. "They usually love him. But they all bet against him not knowing who it was. They're mad because they know he can win."

"And they'll all lose."

"Exactly."

"Do you think he can win?"

"If you don't screw it up, yeah."

I scowl at him. "How would I screw it up?"

He turns to me with serious eyes. "Keep silent. Don't distract him. He knows you're out here watching and that's pressure enough. If he thinks you're in trouble or upset, he'll make a mistake. Let him keep his head in the game. Whatever you see, whatever you hear, keep silent. Don't you dare call out or scream."

"I never scream," I tell him hotly, feeling insulted.

"Well, don't start now. It's about to get ugly."

He's not joking.

The low lights are dimmed further as Ryan is blindfolded with a thick, black cloth. Then a black bag is draped over his head and tied off at the neck. There's no way he can see anything in that cage ringed with Risen. It is the dumbest thing I have ever seen anyone do in my life.

The announcer backs away. The crowd begins to

chant.

"Five!"

Men rush in, grab hold of the shackles holding the Risen in place.

"Four!"

The Risen snap at the men, eager for fresh meat.

"Three!"

A Risen stumbles toward Ryan, reaching for him where he stands in the center of the ring.

"Two!"

He's blind. Defenseless. Surrounded by death and danger.

"One!"

The shackles are released.

The crowd goes insane. They're screaming at the tops of their lungs, banging on the boards beneath us, shaking the ground. I'm terrified by it, but not because I think we'll fall. Not anymore. I'm scared because Ryan is not only blind, he's deaf. No way he can hear the Risen over this chaos echoing throughout the room.

He's going to die. And I'm going to watch.

When the countdown ends, Ryan drops to the ground. He rolls forward across the ground, past the Risen on his right and comes to a stop just shy of the edge of the Arena. People reach in, arms trying to grab him. Probably trying to hold him in place so the Risen can get to him and they can get their drugs, whores, favors or whatever it is they've gambled to gain. Trent says they love him but they'd rather watch him die than lose this game. Even after all these years, with every part of me I've shut down and everything I've lost, I still know what love this. And this isn't it.

"He knows the barriers by heart," Trent leans down to tell me.

He stands so tall above me, I'm sure he has no trouble seeing inside the Arena. There are areas I can't see that are blocked by people's heads. By the shifting, writhing mass around me. I can see two of the three Risen and that third one being a mystery makes me anxious. I can't imagine how Ryan feels not seeing any of them but knowing they're there.

"He knows to stay away from the edges. He's paced that Arena so many times that he has it mapped in his head. He'll never let the living touch him."

"It's the non-living I'm worried about," I grumble.

"It shouldn't be."

Two of the Risen descend on Ryan where he sits crouched, waiting. He must sense them or smell them because he reacts immediately. He lashes out to the right, deftly grabbing a Risen by the ankle and yanking its leg out from under it. It topples onto its back, cracking it's head on the floor. But it doesn't stop moving. Ryan stands quickly, still holding the ankle. He pushes his foot into the Risen's groin, makes a sharp twisting motion and yanks up. The Risen's leg snaps free at the kneecap.

"And he just got himself a weapon," Trent muses proudly.

I don't dare look at him because I'm pretty sure from his tone that he's smiling and no part of me can handle that right now.

The second Risen is creeping up on Ryan's back. I can see the third as well, coming around the far side of the Arena. It's distracted by the people around the edges. It keeps grabbing at them, lunging to get through the barrier but the people are too quick for it.

Ryan takes firm hold of the ankle on the lower leg he's holding, spins around and smacks the Risen behind him in the face. It stumbles but doesn't go down. Reaching out with its gray hands, it grabs for Ryan. He feels its touch, jumps back a step, crouching low again. I watch in horror as he puts the leg on the ground beside him and waits, defenseless again.

The Risen comes at him, lumbering toward him with surprising speed. Ryan immediately tackles it at the knees, standing up and bringing it into the air. Then he spins, bringing the Risen back down to the ground. Hard. Its head bounces off the cement floor, then smacks down again. Ryan lands on top of it, quickly groping for the arms, then pinning them down with his knees. He's straddling the chest as the Risen snaps at him, its arms flailing uselessly to get ahold of him. Ryan moves his hand to the top of the head, carefully feels down the sides until he has hold of the ears, then he jerks the head forward and slams it into the cement again. He rears back, bringing the head with him, then throws all of the weight of his upper body into the movement of smashing the Risen's skull down again. He does it three more times, quick as anything I've ever seen, and the Risen goes slack. Motionless. Completely dead.

One down.

Or actually, two down but one is coming toward him, dragging itself over the ground. A Crawler. I hate Crawlers. Ryan ignores it or doesn't remember it's there, something I don't believe possible after what I've seen so far. Instead of attacking it, he feels around the ground until he finds the leg he dropped. He removes the shoe from the foot and slips it on his own.

I cringe thinking of what the inside of that thing feels or smells like.

With the new, disgusting shoe on his foot, Ryan feels for the Crawler on the ground. His hand gets dangerously close to its mouth, making me gasp.

Trent shoots me a warning look. I glare back.

"Sorry, cyborg. I'm a little worried, it slipped out."

He puts his finger to his lips, silently signaling for me to be quiet.

"Like he could hear me," I say defensively, looking away.

Ryan is now dragging the Crawler to a bench, moving with sure feet as though he can see where he's going. He has the thing by the head and wastes no time putting its face on the edge of the bench. Then he rears back.

"Oh no," I mutter.

"Shhh,"

Ryan stomps on the back of the Risen's head. There's a crack that can't be heard but it's definitely seen. The Risen goes down, lifeless.

One left.

The only problem is, Ryan obviously doesn't know where it is. He tosses aside the Risen he's just finished off, probably to get it's scent away so he smell the next one coming, but it's not working. It's close to him and getting closer. He stays crouched down low beside the bench, using it for some cover and probably to orient himself, but it's making him vulnerable. The Risen is coming up on the other side of the bench, getting ready to lean over it. To grab Ryan by the shoulder.

And he has no idea it's coming.

A shrill whistle sounds beside my ear, making me drop to the ground to defend myself. My left ear, the one beside Trent, is ringing painfully. It sounds again, two short, sharp shrieks. I look up to find Trent watching Ryan closely, his hand over his mouth. I jump up to look for Ryan but nearly drop down again when Trent moves his hand slightly and there's another whistle, this time more pronounced. The two shrieks are slightly longer, more emphatic.

My eyes shoot to the Arena just in time to see Ryan reacting to the Risen closing on his left. He's too late. It gets ahold of his shoulder, it's vice like hands digging its fingers into his flesh. I worry he'll cry out or panic. That he'll lose his bearings because of the pain and it will all be over. But he only slouches slightly, instinctively trying to escape the pain. The he grabs the hand, pulls it toward him and topples the Risen over the bench. He breaks the hold it has on him. With his body free, with his blood pouring bright red and angry down his body, he slides the Risen onto the bench, feeling behind its head until the surface disappears and it's dangling off the edge. Then he lifts his shoed foot and steps down hard. The neck snaps. The Risen is dead.

And with the wound he's taken, there's every chance Ryan will be too.

Chapter Twelve

"Gentleman!" the announcer calls out, appearing in the Arena beside Ryan. "I give you your champion of the Blind! Ryan Hyperion!!!"

There are scattered cheers, losers grudgingly accepting that their winnings are lost but their favorite fighter is still alive. Mostly there's a tense, angry quiet. One that makes my muscles tighten and my skin crawl.

"Time to move," Trent tells me.

He takes my upper arm as he ushers me quickly through the crowd. We jump down off the risers into the dark and head for the exit. He leads me away from the stairs, this time taking me through a different door that leads down an industrial looking hallway with brick walls and exposed wiring in the ceiling.

"Hey, wait," a voice calls quietly from behind us.

I turn to see Elise hurrying toward us, her eyes nervously scanning the hallway.

"Here, take this. You'll need it for his shoulder." She holds out a small bottle and a jar with white paste in it. "Get him out of here now."

"We're already going," Trent tells her, pulling me forward again.

"Thank you," I call over my shoulder, holding up the jar and bottle.

She's turned to leave. If she hears my gratitude, she doesn't acknowledge it.

We jog down the hall until a door slams open ahead of us. The heavy metal door swings noisily, flying out, banging against the brick wall and rebounding back. Trent halts, his body going stiff as he watches. As he waits.

Ryan stumbles out into the hall. He's still in the shorts, no shirt, but luckily the shoe is gone and he's carrying his own pair in his hand along with the rest of his clothes.

"Go, man," a guy says gruffly from inside the door. "Get out before it gets nuts in here. Don't come back for a while either. People will forget but not any time soon."

Ryan leans back against the wall, his head falling forward as he nods. "Hopefully I'm never coming back."

"That's what everyone says. Ask me how many times it happens?"

"Thanks for the help," Ryan says in reply, wearily leaning forward and extending his hand.

A guy steps out to slap it once quickly with his. He spots us, his eyes locking on mine and I realize it's the guy that led us inside Marlow's office. The second bouncer. He hesitates for a second looking like he wants to say something, but then he quickly pulls the door closed and slams it behind him.

"Good show," Trent tells Ryan.

He looks up at us with a wan smile, his face flushed and his hair flying wet and dark in every direction. I'm wound so tight, so freaked out and so relieved to see him alive that I lose my mind a little. Maybe a lot.

I run at him down the hall, pushing past Trent. Ryan sees me coming. His eyes go wide with surprise but he stands up straight, opening his arms to me. I'm a jerk because I know he's tired. I know he's hurt. But I'm selfish. I jump at him, wrapping my arms around his neck, my legs around his waist and I cling to him hard. If I don't do this, if I don't hold on to him and reassure myself that he's alright, I'll cry. And I am sick to death of that feeling. As it is, I bury my face in his neck, worried the tears will come anyway.

"I'm bleeding on you," he says softly, his arms wound tightly around me, hugging me to him.

"Good. It means you have a heartbeat."

I need to let him go. We need to get out of here now, but first we have to deal with his shoulder. Who knows what fluids the Risen might have gotten inside him. The sickness doesn't move nearly as fast as it used to, but an infection is still an infection. You shouldn't mess with a corpse, whether it's lying in a pine box or trying to sink its teeth into your eye.

"I have stuff for your shoulder."

"It can wait." He squeezes me tighter.

"No, it can't."

"Joss, how often do you let me hold you?"

I sigh against his skin. "Never."

"Then let me have this."

So I do. And it doesn't hurt me to do it. It doesn't make me anxious or twitchy. I don't feel smothered even as I rebreathe my own hot air rebounding off his neck. He smells exactly as his bed did. Soap, sweat and dude. Like a man. A man who isn't afraid to fight with me. For me. Who'd risk his life to keep safe something sacred that I very rarely thought about, not beyond keeping it hidden. Not until this moment when so much of his skin is hot against mine, when my body is wound around him like it was built to be here, made to hold to him. To be held against him. Now I'm wondering what better way there is to make sure it's never stolen, never taken away like everything else that was ever mine, than to give it to someone. Someone who's patient. Strong. Understanding. Someone who knows it's worth so much more than a Benjamin, that you could never put a price on it, that it's not rare because it's hard to come by. It's rare because it's me. The last of me.

"Ryan," Trent says, his voice a warning.

"I know," he replies reluctantly.

He loosens his hold on me, lets me slide down his body slowly until I'm on my own two foot but I'm looking up at him with everything I've been thinking on my face. I could hide it. I know how. But I don't. I let him see it and I watch his breathing change as he does. As he understands. And I know he's thinking about it now too.

"Shoulder," I say firmly, pulling away.

I hand him the stuff Elise gave me. He quickly uncorks the bottle and downs the entire thing in one long gulp.

"What is that?" I ask.

He grimaces as he finishes it, swiping the back of his hand across his mouth.

"You don't want to know."

He tosses the bottle aside, letting it shatter on the brick wall farther down the hall.

"Oh, okay. That's… littering."

"Are you going to write me a ticket? Screw this place. Let's get out of here."

He leads us out a door that takes us up a flight of stairs to a blackened hallway. No lights at all in here. Ryan and Trent must know the layout, though, because when Ryan takes my hand, he leads me quickly through the dark without banging us into anything. I'm starting to wonder how much time these two have spent in this place.

Finally we burst out a side door into the cold night. The sky is dark, cloudy. The wind coming off the water is frigid and I worry about Ryan in just the shorts they put him in as he runs us down the worn, gray boards of the pier to the end of the building.

"Let's see if Marlow is true to his word," he says as we reach the end.

When we look down, we all stare silently.

There in the water tied to the pier is a small sailboat. Mast, sails and all.

"Captain Hook boned us!" I exclaim.

"What?" Ryan asks.

"It's the Jolly friggin' Roger."

"It's a daysailer," Trent says sadly, looking it over.

"How do you know that?"

"I read."

"What? Back issues of Yacht Club Weekly while you're on the toilet?"

He grins at me. "I like sailing adventures. Pirates. Buccaneers. I got your Jolly Roger joke. *Peter Pan.* It was funny."

I sigh. "I'm still mad at you."

"For what?"

"For knowing everything," Ryan says, glaring down at our boat.

It's just over ten feet long and can't be more than five feet wide. The three of us in this boat is going to be interesting. The fact that I doubt any of us know how to sail a sailboat is going to be a tragedy.

"Can you sail one, Trent?" Ryan asks hopefully.

He chuckles. "No."

"Yeah, me either."

"Well, whatever," I say, throwing my hands in the air. "Marlow's a dick, but it is a boat so let's at least see if we can figure it out. How hard can it be? You hoist the sails, they catch the wind, and we cruise across the water. There's a rudder, I think. We steer with that? We'll figure it out once we're out on open water."

"Sounds solid and not at all suicidal. Let's do it."

Once we untie the boat, or cast off or whatever it is, Trent gets to work figuring out the riggings and sails while I apply the white paste to Ryan's shoulder. He's changed back into his own pants and shoes, tossing the shorts into the water as we drift.

"How worried should I be?" I ask as I smear a huge glob on the worst of his wounds. This stuff smells like it stings.

"Not very," he replies tightly. "I saw the Risen when they took the hood off. Its fingers were nothing but dry bone. That's why it was able to dig into my skin so deep."

"Did they do that to it on purpose?"

"I don't think so. They keep them locked up in cages or cells in the building until they need them for a fight. That's days or weeks of the Risen wandering around an empty room looking for a way out. They claw at the walls and if those walls are brick or cement, the skin will give out first."

"I got it," Trent says triumphantly.

He yanks a cord and I watch in amazement as a brilliant white sail raises sharply. It whips in the wind, fluttering bright against the dark sky until Trent pulls another cord, tying it off quickly while he grabs the rudder. There's a *snap* above us as the sheet takes hold of the wind and then we're off, jerking back toward the docks and the aquarium.

Trent curses, adjusts the rudder and another line. Soon we're changing course, heading out into the Sound and dipping south. We'll have to pass by the docks just outside the stadiums, but I'm sure Trent will swing us wide. Though our bright white sail makes us a little hard to miss, even in the dark.

I pat Ryan on the back twice, letting him know I'm done and he puts his shirt back on.

"Trent, you looked at the map. What is this island really? What was it before?" I ask. Now that all of the other threats (Marlow, his men, the Risen in the Arena) are fading small behind us, I'm focusing on the biggest, newest one. The unknown.

"It used to be called Vashon Island, thus the group's name. People lived there. It was mostly residential with small farming. There are no bridges to it which is probably why the Vashons chose it. It was always isolated with good farm land. Easily self-sufficient in the right hands."

"Crenshaw's kind of people would be the right hands, I guess."

"Why did you ask me what it really is? What did Crenshaw say it was? Narnia?"

I grin, happy I get the reference. "Elysium."

Trent nods, the wind whipping his hair across his eyes. He squints against it and leans casually on the rudder. He looks every bit the sailor then. I think I should tell him that, that it might make him happy to know he's living his dream, but then I sees several flashes of light behind him and my heart begins to race.

"Hey, guys," I whisper. "I think I saw something."

Ryan turns to see what I'm looking at. Trent keeps his eyes forward.

"What was it?" Ryan asks, his voice also hushed.

"There was light on the bank. Right there."

I point to the shore a little bit south of the stadiums.

"What kind of light? Like a fire?"

"More like a signal." I look at Trent, catching his eye. "Organized. Like they knew what they were doing."

Not like they were desperate, grasping at straws in a last ditch attempt not to die on a roof surrounded by Risen.

"It's probably the Colonies," he tells me calmly. "They run constant patrols around the perimeter of the stadiums. Someone may have been signaling the all clear."

"Or they could have been telling someone there's a boat cruising through the Sound."

He shrugs. "And?"

"And they could come after us," I snap, my voice rising.

"Gasoline is gone. They'll have to row or sail like we are. They won't catch up to us. You worry too much."

"Is that a joke?"

He smiles, but I don't know if that means yes, that's a joke or that he's happy he pushed my buttons. Either way, he's annoying me.

"We'll be alright, Joss," Ryan tells me. "If they come after us, we'll go ashore and hide."

"We'll lose Marlow's boat."

Ryan snorts. "I'm planning on burning it when we're done with it anyway."

Chapter Thirteen

"Why do you hate *Pretty in Pink*?" Ryan asks me out of nowhere, his quiet voice breaking the silence we've been sailing in.

I grin, my eyes staying lazily fixed on the rippling surface of the water in the moonlight. It's hypnotic, like fire.

"Because the girl is an idiot."

"We're all idiots when it comes to love," Trent says philosophically.

I glance back at him, surprised. He smiles at me with is creepy, real boy smile on his Pinocchio face.

"Why was she an idiot?" Ryan asks, ignoring Trent.

"Because she chose the wrong guy to love. It makes me angry."

"We don't choose who we love, love chooses us," Trent tells me.

I turn fully around to face him. "What is with you?"

"Nothing. Are we not discussing this?"

"Discussing what?"

"Love."

"No," I reply quickly, not sure why I feel embarrassed by the word.

"We're talking about the movie," Ryan tells Trent pointedly.

"That's what I was talking about," Trent insists.

"No," I tell him, shaking my head. "You were talking about real life and I'm beginning to wonder just what kind of nautical adventures you're reading? Are they the type with half naked women falling over the arm of a shirtless pirate kind of 'adventure'?"

"You mean lady porn?"

"No!"

"That's what you were describing," Ryan says.

"No, it's not."

"Do you read lady porn?" Trent asks calmly.

I pause to cool down, to collect myself and not give anything away. To get angrier is to be too adamant in my denials and they'll never believe me. And they'll know that, yes, I do have lady porn. Sue me!

"Anyway," I say tightly, "I get annoyed with *Pretty in Pink* because her best friend is in love with her but she brushes him off to date some rich guy who then brushes her off for his friends because they're snobs and they look down on her because she's all poor and crap."

Ryan frowns. "That's the whole movie? *Sixteen Candles* was way better."

"Of course it was, but that's not the end of the movie. The guy comes groveling back, apologizing for sucking and her best friend forgives her even though he still loves her and everyone lives happily ever after. Everyone but the friend. It's stupid. She chose the wrong guy."

Ryan nods thoughtfully. "Can I just hate it with you instead of committing two hours of my life to watching it?"

"No, it's all or nothing. You have to feel the anger, Ryan. You have to live it with me to really appreciate the hate. You have to yell at the screen and tell her she's dumb."

"You can't hate by proxy," Trent agrees. "That's lazy."

"Can't we watch *Sixteen Candles* again?" Ryan pleads.

I shake my head. "Not until you live the hate."

"Lame."

"No, you know what's lame? Watching you cage fight three Risen *blindfolded*."

That right there, that's a mic drop. That's an end of discussion because there's no coming back from that and smart guy that he is, Ryan knows it.

After almost an hour of sailing, we see light in the distance. Nothing direct, just the yellow haze of civilization spread out and thriving. It's the burn of electric life humming in the perfect darkness of a world gone dead. It's strange. Eerie. And we're headed right for it. I feel anxious. Like we're headed somewhere I used to know but forgot about. Somewhere I'm not so sure I want to go again.

I glance at the Lost Boy ahead of me, then at the one behind me as the tall white sail snaps in the cold air above us. I want to tell them to turn the ship around, to take me back to Neverland.

I want to tell them I'm not ready for this.

"This is weird," Ryan whispers.

"I don't like it," I agree.

Something floating in the water smacks the hull of the boat, startling us all. We fly past it, fast on the wind, but I look back to see a large, round object floating in the water. It's painted hot pink.

"What was that?" I ask.

"Buoy," Trent answers, his eyes fixed steadily forward. "Fair warning, there are more coming."

He's not kidding. We pass by another not long after. This one is bright green. Then a yellow. A blue. A white.

"What are they marking?"

"Water depth?" Ryan suggests.

"Maybe," Trent says, not sounding convinced.

If he plans on telling us what he thinks they are marking, he never gets the chance. We're nearing the shore. I can see it building in front of us, a black mass against the dark sky. The lights glow from far inside the island, but out here there's nothing. Nothing but the strange buoys, the sound of the water lapping against the shore and the group of men standing submerged up to their knees in it with weapons in hand.

They appear out of nowhere. Shadows in black stepping out of the night, waiting patiently with clubs, spears and machetes held confidently. These weapons haven't seen the constant use ours do in the city, but it doesn't mean they don't know how to use them. You can see it in the way they hold them. These are still hunters. Killers, as we all now have to be because we no longer have the luxury of someone else doing the dirty work for us. Military, police, hunters, farmers. Everyone who took lives for our safety and comfort are dead and gone. Or they're us now. I wonder what I'd classify as, other than scared.

This is a huge unknown, sitting in this Hive boat in front of a group of mysterious men on an island I've never heard of. One that Marlow was way too interested in yet unwilling to approach himself. One that Crenshaw helped build once upon a time. One that he calls Elysium, Heaven, but that right now feels more like something sinister and better left forgotten.

Trent drops our sails. I'm surprised how quickly we

lose momentum. I'm thrown forward, right into Ryan's back. He doesn't look back but he reaches for me subtly, keeping his movements hidden in the hull of the boat. I weave my fingers through his until our hands are loosely tangled together. I'm shocked by how much that small contact actually helps. How steadier I feel.

"You're lost," a man calls out calmly.

"Is this Vashon island?" Trent calls in reply.

"It was."

"What is it now?" I ask.

I can feel eyes on me. It's my voice. It just told them I'm a girl and I wonder what that changes for them. If it puts me in more danger or less.

"Nothing for you. Turn this boat around and go back the way you came."

"We came looking for help."

"You came to the wrong place."

"That's not what Crenshaw said," I say clearly, playing the only card we have and hoping it lands.

"I don't know what a crenshaw is and I don't care," he says, his voice turning cold. "Turn it around. Leave."

"No."

He takes a step closer, his machete cutting through the water as he approaches. I can see him better now. He's stocky. Strong. Probably about 30 or so but he looks young enough, healthy enough, to be a problem for me with my messed up arm and an exhausted Ryan with an injured shoulder. I realize as I watch him approach that it was a big mistake coming here like this. In the dead of night in a boat full of injured people with no clear idea of how we'll convince them to help us. Everything with The Hive happened so fast, we didn't take time to think this through. To plan. But we're in it now and there's no going back.

I swing my feet out of the boat, slipping off the side to land in the water. I stifle the gasp that begs to explode out of me when my body registers the cold. I'm only in it up to my thighs, but it's enough to make me want out. Cold and wet means sick and dead in my mind.

"They'll leave, but I'm staying," I tell him, working to keep the tightness out of my voice. "We need help. I want to talk to your leader."

"Joss, we're not leaving you here," Ryan insists angrily.

"He's right, because you're all leaving," the guy agrees.

I hold out my hands, pressing my wrists together firmly. "I'm not. You're taking me with you back to your camp or whatever it is you have here. You can bind my hands and search me if you want, but you're taking me back with you. Either that or I'm walking out of this water onto that beach and you'll have to kill me to stop me."

The guy looks at my wrists pressed together. He smirks. "I didn't bring my handcuffs with me. Sorry."

"You're also not completely stupid. You don't leave the house without a weapon, a piece of flint and a rope of some kind."

His smirk becomes a scowl. "We don't live like that anymore. I'd like to keep it that way, which is why you're leaving."

I step toward him. "Not until I talk to someone."

He glares at him, his eyes shining hard in the faint moonlight. I'm beginning to shiver from the cold. From the wet, and I don't know when or where I'll get a chance to dry off and warm up. That scares me more than anything.

"Please," I say softly, my eyes imploring.

I see it when he sighs. When he decides to help me. I wonder if it's because I'm a girl or if it's because he remembers what it was like to be me out in the crazy or if it's just because he's cold too and wants to get back inside. I don't know and I don't care. What matters is that he nods reluctantly, gestures for some of his boys to come to the boat to secure my boys and leads me up to shore.

"Do you have any weapons on you?" he asks, sounding bored and annoyed.

I nod, seeing no point in lying. I'll be searched anyway. It's then that it dawns on me that I was never searched going inside The Hive. Even to speak to Marlow. I remind myself to ask Ryan about it later.

"An ASP," I tell the guy, "and a knife."

"Take 'em out. Toss 'em on the ground over there."

I do as he says. I can hear Trent and Ryan being asked to do the same with whatever they have. Farther up on the shore, three men with crossbows watch us all patiently, their weapons raised and ready.

"Is that it? Nothing else you want to tell me about?"

I shake my head. "That's it."

"I'm going to frisk you now. If I find any surprises, you're getting your knife back in your chest. Got it?"

"Got it."

He searches me carefully. It's not the obscenely thorough inspection I got from the Colonists, but it's for real. He's quick. He never lingers inappropriately anywhere, but his hands touch me in places that no guy has ever touched me before. I'm tense, having to remind myself over and over again not to punch him in the throat. Finally, when I'm blushing and shaking from more than the cold, he steps away. When I meet his eyes, they're tight but apologetic. Good to know he feels as weird about what just happened as I do.

He picks up my weapons then gestures for me to walk up the bank. I hear him fall in step behind me a few paces back. He's giving himself space between us. Breathing room in case I try anything.

"That way," a guy with a crossbow tells me, gesturing with his weapon.

I follow his directions, cutting left to walk along the shore. I hear them all walking loudly at my back and it makes me sick to my stomach but I don't turn around. I don't make any unnecessary moves. First, it's dark and I can't really see where I'm going. Second, I don't want to get shot.

Eventually they guide us inland on a well-worn path that drops us in a parking lot. There are several abandoned cars, all parked with such orderly precision in the faded white lines that it makes me anxious. Chaos I can understand. This is just weird.

We walk for quite awhile in perfect silence, the sound of our feet on the dirt packed earth the only break. That and the crickets. It sounds like they're everywhere, something that freaks me out. I can't listen for the sound of approaching Risen in the brush over the noise of theses bugs and the constant crunch of so many men's feet behind me. But then I guess there might not be any Risen here. That, like the straight lines in the parking lot, makes me anxious and angry.

Eventually we walk along an old driveway until we meet a fence. One of the guys goes up to it, speaks into a gray box and a few seconds later the black iron creaks, groans and swings open slowly. Once we're ushered inside, I look over my shoulder to watch the gate clang shut behind us. It's tall and imposing, but push come to shove, I'm pretty sure I could climb it. I will absolutely *not* be held captive again.

This area is all open field. There are trees scattered around the edges of the property, but for as far as I can see there are fences. There's also the dark shape of a building looming in the distance, a scattering of lights on in each floor. I start to sweat thinking of all the people probably bustling inside. How many are sleeping in a huge room full of beds? How many will swarm us the second we walk in the door? How many voices and bodies will bombard me for the next few hours or days that I'm stuck here trying to do the impossible?

By the time we reach the front door of the large brown house, I'm ready to turn and run. To try my luck on scaling that fence and head for the water. When the door swings open and light spills out onto the porch, shining in my eyes like the sun, I hesitate. I don't want to do this again. It's different, sure, but a lot of it is the same. I don't know what to expect in here. I don't know anything about these people at all. Maybe they're like the cannibals out there in the wild, feasting on other healthy, living humans. Hunting them for the sport of it. Maybe I'll end up dinner or maybe we'll become science experiments.

What happens is we're greeted with silence. A large empty entrance hall with tall ceilings, a huge staircase and absolutely no people. I'm nudged from behind to get me moving and the amazing thing is that I go without protest. It's warm, light and quiet. It's dry. It's empty. It has pictures on the walls, a decent rug over the hard floor. It smells like hot food.

It feels like a real home.

I glance back at Ryan to see him looking around in awe, his face saying everything I'm thinking. This is unreal. This is a step back in time to before the beginning. Before the bad days. Before we lost everything and everyone. He meets my eyes for the briefest of moments before we're ushered farther inside and his expression reflects my own – it's terrifying.

"In here," the stocky guy tells me. "You're going into quarantine in the back."

"All of us together?" I ask, feeling my pulse quicken.

If their cleansing practices are anything like the Colonies, I can't handle having Trent and Ryan in the same room seeing that. Maybe these people are bigger animals than I took them for.

"Yeah, of course. Sorry we don't have separate rooms but your modesty will just have to survive it, princess."

I bristle at being called princess, reminded of the first time I met Ryan when he called me the same thing. I sleep on a pile of rags on the floor like Cinder-freaking-rella. How exactly am I princess here?

We're led down the hall to the back of the house. I hear movement inside as we go. Hurried footsteps on the floor above us, a door shutting quickly. Somewhere in a kitchen nearby a pot or pan is banged against another. I'm trying to get a count on how many people are here but I'm sure I'm not getting all of them. I wonder if this is their main house where most of the people live or if we're being held somewhere completely isolated. Judging by the open fields around the house, I'm thinking isolated.

"Inside," Stocky tells me, opening a door to a dark room.

I glare at him as I walk past, not flinching at walking into an unknown, unlit room. I've been through worse and I want him to know it. To know that I'm no princess. That I've got backbone for miles.

When he flicks on the light, I'm shocked. This house keeps doing that to me. These people keep doing that. It's a library, full of books on nearly every single wall but it's really surprise attraction is the cage. It's built against one of the walls, the bars going nearly to the ceiling. It's something I'm thinking they stole from a police station. Something they carefully tore down and built up back here in this house. Inside there's a single twin bed with sheets on a real mattress and a comforter. They don't match but I'm not judging.

I look at Stocky to find him impatiently gesturing me forward, toward the cage.

"Seriously?" I ask him in amazement. "You're just going to lock us in there? No showers? No scrubbing? No lice shampoo?"

He scowls at me. "No, no showers. No steam treatments either. The hotel spa is closed at the moment but if the accommodations are not up to your standards I can look into getting you moved to another wing. Do you want me to see if the Presidential Suite is available? Do you need turn down service? Perhaps a shoe shine."

I scowl right back. "I don't know what any of that means."

"It means this is the quarantine room, get inside," he says gruffly. "I know there's only one bed but we'll bring two more mattresses down. We aren't exactly used to having guests. I'm so sorry."

"Okay, the sarcasm I understand."

"Great. I'm fluent in it. Now for the last time, get in the cage or get out. My dinner is getting colder the longer I'm standing here gabbing with you."

"Come on, Joss," Ryan says, stepping between Stocky and I.

I follow him into the cage, feeling Trent close on my heels. They clang the metal door shut behind us and that's that. We're locked in. Prisoners. But for how long? And why doesn't it feel the same? Why doesn't it make me ill the way the Colony did? I'm more locked down here than I ever was there but it doesn't make me stir crazy.

I'm about to ask how long our quarantine will last when Stocky gives us the rundown.

"Listen up, here's the deal," he says, sounding bored. "This is the quarantine area. This will be your home for the next two weeks."

"Two weeks?" I exclaim.

Stocky holds up his hand. "Please hold all questions until the end of the tour. You are not prisoners here. If at any time you want to leave, you are free to go. I would actually prefer it if you left so give it some serious thought. If you choose to stay, you will remain in quarantine for the two week period. After that, if you do not turn into flesh eating zombies, you will be released from quarantine and brought before a council. This council will decide what to do with you. Getting through the quarantine does not guarantee you anything. In two weeks the council may decide to deport you immediately at which time you will be put right back on your little boat and sent on your way with a reminder to never come back. This is the most likely scenario, so I ask you again to consider saving both you and I a whole lot of time and hassle and leave immediately. No pressure. Speaking of pressure, through that door behind you is the bathroom. I assume you've seen one before. Maybe even operated a toilet or two in your day, but I don't have high hopes. Please do not defecate on the floor. Use the toilet. I wish I didn't have to say this, but experience has taught me otherwise." He looks directly at me. "There is a shower with soap and hot water, clean towels, but sadly no facial masks, exfoliants or cucumber slices for your weary eyes. My sincerest apologies."

I narrow my eyes at him. "I asked if you were going to scrub us down like the Colonies, I didn't exactly ask for a massage."

He pauses, sizing me up, seeming to take in my clothing and appearance in detail for the first time. "How exactly do you know what the Colony does to new members?"

I freeze, realizing my mistake. I worried insanely that Ryan and Trent would think I was a Colonist spy, that I hadn't escaped but that I'd been a member all along. To these people that don't know me at all, that worry doesn't seem so insane.

"I've heard stories," I tell him.

He continues to watch me silently. I stare back, desperate not to look guilty of anything but I just flat out lied so I'm feeling pretty boldly guilty at the moment.

"I'm going to eat my dinner," he finally says, his voice turning low and serious. He's no longer the bored, sarcastic tour guide anymore. He's very alert. Very aware of me. "You'll get yours soon enough. The extra mattresses too. In the meantime, don't get too comfortable."

With that he's gone, he and his entire entourage. It's just me, Ryan and Trent in the cage in the library in the building in the wild on an island emptied of Risen.

Chapter Fourteen

"Is prison supposed to be nicer than home?" Trent asks, glancing over the book spines on the shelves.

"Didn't you hear?" Ryan asks drolly. "It's not a prison."

"Awful lot of bars for 'not a prison,'" I mutter.

"Joss, you take the bed. I don't know if they'll make good on the promise of other mattresses but even if they don't Trent and I will be fine on the floor."

"I can sleep on the floor."

"We all can sleep on the floor," Trent says. "No one is saying you can't. But it's not very chivalrous for either of us to take the bed with a girl in the mix."

"So you're saying we're all equal, but I'm a girl so I get the bed?"

"Doesn't make any sense, does it?" He shrugs. "Maybe that's why chivalry is dead. It's dumb."

"It's not dead and it's not dumb," Ryan protests sounding tired and annoyed. "She's taking the bed. Can we not make it an issue? Can you just say 'thank you' and lay down?"

"Can I go to the bathroom first?" I ask quietly, surprised by his sharp tone.

"Ryan, you sound exhausted. You should take a nap," Trent suggests. He snaps his fingers like he just had a brilliant idea. "The bed! Why don't you take it? Lie down? Joss, you don't mind, right?"

Ryan runs his hands over his face, groaning. "Not now. Seriously so much, not now, dude."

Trent frowns at the bed. "There's no mint on this pillow."

"I'm going to the bathroom," I mumble, leaving them to work it out.

Inside the small room behind the library is a gleaming white, sterile as balls bathroom that makes me afraid to touch anything. This is familiar. This feels like the Colonies. Everything wiped down, everything in its place, the faint hint of anal retentive douchebaggery hanging in the air. And Stocky didn't lie. There's a shower that has steaming hot running water with clean towels that smell like soap and something else. Something flowery that I don't like but it's not mildew so I'll roll with it. There's soap in the shower as well. Something a lot like the Colony soap but with a slightly different scent. More of the flowers, I think. It's smoother too. More like a lotion. It's nice.

It's then that I realize I'm naked in the shower under the hot water, my dirty, wet clothes a sodden pile on the perfect white floor. I honestly don't know how I ended up in here covered in lavender scented lather. There was no conscious decision to do it, it just… happened. Too late to turn back now.

I stay in for ten minutes, washing my hair and body once per minute. I would stay in and do it all again if I wasn't worried about letting the guys have a go at it. I'm trying not to be selfish, to think of others every now and then, but it's hard because I desperately want it all for myself. As I climb reluctantly out the warm shower into the chilled air, I decide that being civilized sucks.

Dressed in my cold wet clothes again, I head back out to the cage. I'm surprised to find the boys' mattresses have arrived and we're not alone. A cot has been set up on the far side of the room near the door where a blond haired guy about my age is covering it in a blanket. It's another comforter. Another genuine blanket that looks clean. Like it would smell of the lavender soap.

He glances up when I come out, giving me a sharp nod. "'Sup?"

I glance at Ryan, unsure.

"This is Sam. He's our guard for the night," Ryan explains.

He's sitting on the floor on his mattress looking like he's ready to tip over. I don't know why he doesn't just go to sleep already.

"I thought we weren't in a prison. Why do we need a guard?"

"In case you decide you want to leave," Sam says, sitting down on his bed with his back against the wall of books. "Taylor is all about you having easy access to the exit at all times."

"Taylor is the stocky guy?"

"Yeah. He's head of security. Whenever we have visitors, which lately is never, he's in charge of making sure they don't cause any problems." Sam smiles at me. "You're messing up his routine right now. He hates you."

"Great."

Our chances of getting to talk to someone important here seem slim to none. I'm not exactly anxious to wait out this two week period just for the chance to talk to a council, but it might be our only option.

I sit down heavily beside Ryan, getting so close that

our sides touch. He glances over at me and smiles weakly, dark crescents forming under his tired eyes.

"You need to sleep," I whisper to him.

He shakes his head, his smile fading. He turns to Sam. "So you're part of security?"

"Yep."

"You seem kind of young for that."

Sam snorts. "What are you? Like a year older than me? You seem kind of young too. Or is it because you grew up on the outside so you think you're tougher than I am?"

"Mostly that."

"Whatever," Sam says, sounding angry. "I grew up in it too. We weren't always this safe. I was in the first quarantine zone when it first started going down."

"So was I. Woodburn, Oregon. You?"

Sam eyes him shrewdly. I'm sure he's wondering if he can believe him.

"Albany."

"Longview, Washington," Trent says absently. He's sitting in the corner in a chair with a book in his hands, his head hovering over it. He's barely listening to us but that's probably still more focus than the average person.

"Seattle," I say softly.

"You were outside it when it started," Sam says. He's not asking. He knows. We all know. We all remember, even all these years later, exactly where the lines were drawn. The cities that they encompassed that mean nothing now. That are dead and buried. Forgotten.

"Yeah," I admit, feeling a little like an outsider. Like somehow even though I lost everything just like they did, I didn't suffer as much because I was spared a few more months of normal. I got one more summer of being a kid, of being carefree and happy. Of swimming pools, popsicles and bike rides. I was given more time, no matter how meager that time feels now. "It didn't reach us until December, back when the secondary quarantines broke down as they started testing the cure."

"The cure," Sam mutters with disgust. "What a load."

"They never fully tested it," Trent says, turning a page. "They made one small breakthrough, announced it as the end of the disease, expanded the quarantine to give it a go and lost control when it turned out it didn't cure anything. It just delayed it. But it wasn't their fault."

"Then whose fault was it?" Ryan asks.

"The people on the outside."

"Excuse me?" I ask hotly.

"Yeah, like you," Trent says, finally looking up from his book. "You and your parents."

"My dead parents? That's who you blame for the fake cure?!"

"Not them specifically," he replies calmly, "but everyone on the outside played a part. They were demanding a cure be found. They were terrified the sickness would get out and kill everyone else on the planet. It was either find a cure or firebomb the entire quarantine zone, something they had started to do. They tried it out to see how the public, how you and your parents, responded to it."

"Portland," Ryan says darkly.

I don't dare look at him. I can feel the anger rolling off him as he thinks about this, as he talks about a time I don't even like to remember let alone speak of. I'm worried some of that anger he's feeling is directed at me, as though I as an eight year old girl contributed to the hell he went through during those first few months.

"You can't blame the people on the outside," I tell Trent defensively. "We were just as clueless as you."

"I didn't say it was entirely your fault, but the pressure the world was putting on the doctors and scientists to get that cure was unreal. It was too much. They rushed it and we all paid for it. Luckily, those of us already on the inside knew how to survive it. Didn't really change our world too much other than the gates were flung open and we were free to roam."

"Only it was better not to," Sam says, "so we were still trapped."

"Were you in one of the Safe Zones?" Ryan asks him.

Sam nods. "Warm Springs down in eastern Oregon. That's where most of us here are from."

"How many people are here?" I ask.

He shrugs. "I don't know. Almost 3,000 I think. When Warm Springs fell apart most of us came here and some others joined us later, but a lot of people bailed. Followed the psycho."

I frown. "Who are you talking about?"

Sam looks at me like he thinks I'm messing with him. I glance at Ryan and Trent to see if they know something I don't, but they look as confused as I feel.

"You guys really don't know, do you?"

I shake my head, see the boys do the same.

"Wow, maybe you really aren't Colonists."

"We're not," I insist angrily.

"Taylor says you know stuff, though. Insider stuff."

"Yeah, because I was inside a Colony as a prisoner," I blurt out, deciding to go for the truth since my lie was weak anyway.

"And you got out?" Sam asks skeptically.

"Barely. The people inside, they feel just as trapped as I did. They helped me escape so I could get help and come back to free them too."

"Please," Sam spits, scowling at me, "they love it in there. They'd follow their Messiah to the ends of the earth and back."

"What Messiah?" Trent asks, suddenly very interested in us.

"The psycho."

"Who are you talking about?" Ryan demands.

Sam looks at me. "You say you were on the inside, how do you not know this? He's the leader of the Colonies. He founded them. The people, they practically worship him and all his crap about keeping everyone clean and pure, about how the Fever was retribution from God for all of the evil in the world and only the righteous will survive. That's why they lock themselves inside so tightly, it's why they cruise the streets *saving* people."

"Who is this guy? Who are you talking about?" Ryan asks again.

"Dr. Westbrook."

"Who is Dr. Westbrook?" I ask. "Should that name mean something to me?"

"Probably not, no. You weren't at Warm Springs. He was a doctor there," Sam says bitterly. "A dentist, actually. He sucked. Anyway, when the second quarantine failed and the Fever started turning the entire world into zombies, Dr. Westbrook started going on and on about how it was right, how God had planned it. How the pure should be kept pure and the wicked would get theirs. He said because we were inside the Safe Zone when it broke the second time that we had been chosen. That no one else should be let in. That they should all be left to die because that's what God wanted. He really went nuts. I heard him talking a few times as a kid and even then I knew it was creepy. But a lot of people agreed with him, which I don't get at all."

"They were afraid," Trent says quietly. "They didn't know what to do, what to believe. The government had failed to protect them so they turned to another higher power. They turned to God. This doctor was promising them that God had chosen them to survive and it gave them hope so they ran with it." He shakes his head sadly. "They just ran a little too far."

Sam nods in agreement, his anger fading. "Eventually everyone that was creeped out by the psycho got out. We formed a separate group and started looking for a new place to live. We needed a new Safe Zone. This island fit the bill."

"Weren't there people already here?" I ask.

"Yeah, lots. Luckily a lot of them were farmers that had been living and working here already. We came in, made a deal that we would help them clear it of the zombies if they helped us learn to live here."

"You people keep saying that," I interrupt.

Sam frowns. "Saying what?"

"'Zombies'. That's an old word isn't it? From horror movies and mythology. I mean, I use it sometimes but almost everyone on the outside in the wild calls them Risen."

Sam chuckles. "Don't let Taylor hear you say that. He already thinks you're a Colonist and that's their word. Westbrook came up with it. It's biblical. Some kind of reference to Lazarus who was actually a good guy so I don't get how it works, but that's what the Colonists all call them. Risen."

Ryan glances at me. "What does Crenshaw call

them? Devils?"

"He makes me call them Wraiths."

He grins. "Nice. I like it."

Trent leans back in his seat, putting his book on a nearby table. "So your people came in and wiped out the zombies then that was it? You were just allowed to stay and live fat off the farmers work after that?"

"No," Sam replies, sounding offended. "We had a lot of really smart people with us in our group from Warm Springs. A lot of military from one of the outposts too. People who knew how to use water to make power and all that. People who knew how to fight. The farmers were happy to have us."

"Better you than the Colonists," I say, trying to smooth over the feathers Trent ruffled.

"Yeah," Sam agrees. "Those people were glad to see us go. They thought that if we were willing to leave the Safe Zone, then we were just as damned as everyone else. They even tried to kill a few people before we got out. People that Westbrook said were tainted."

The door swings open, startling everyone. Stocky, or Taylor as Sam calls him, comes in with three plates carefully balanced in his arms. He nods to Sam.

"You wanna open the door for me so I can pass them their dinner?"

Sam jumps up. "You got it."

"It's nothing special. Mashed potatoes, some pot roast, carrots," he rattles off, looking right at me. "Couldn't find filet mignon, sorry. And the house wine is water. You'll find it on tap in the bathroom. Or the toilet, whichever you prefer."

"We'll just have to make due, I suppose," I tell him bitingly. "Hopefully the desert will make up for the dinner."

"I'll see what I can find special, just for you."

"Joss," Trent calls to me, "if he brings you anything chocolate, don't eat it."

"I'll keep that in mind. Thanks, Trent."

"You're welcome."

After that, after we eat and Taylor leaves us alone with Sam again with strict orders for quiet and lights out, we go to bed. Ryan pulls his mattress up close to the bed, positioning himself on the floor between me and the cage door. I don't say anything when he does it. If it helps him sleep better, I want him to do it even if I don't think I need protecting. Even if I don't want to need it. I wait, lying perfectly still and silent, until I hear Ryan start to snore. It doesn't take long. He's had a long day. One I'm going to try my hardest to forget because despite what an impressive fighter he is, watching him in that arena was gruesome, morbid and terrifying. My heart has stopped and run faster than it ever should more times tonight than I want to think about. I also don't want to think about what that means. That it's all for him. That my heartbeats are tied to his, carried away and brought to a standstill by his actions. By his wellbeing. By his smiles.

Chapter Fifteen

"Joss," Ryan whispers sharply.

Gentle hands shake me roughly.

"Joss, wake up."

I pry my tired eyes open, trying to bring them to focus. To make sense of the Ryan shaped shadow forcing me awake.

"Wh-what's happening? What's wrong?"

"You were talking in your sleep."

"She was moaning in her sleep," Trent says, his voice muffled and distant.

"I got this," Ryan tells him. "Go back to sleep."

"Gladly."

I run my hand over my eyes. My fingers come away wet.

"I was moaning?"

"And whimpering," Sam calls from across the room.

Ryan drops his forehead against my shoulder. "I said I got it, man."

"Only trying to help."

"I'm sorry, guys," I whisper, feeling horrified. Ryan is sugar coating it. I was crying in my sleep.

"Don't be," Sam says.

"Do you want to talk about it?" Trent asks, his

words almost indiscernible. I think his face is seriously planted in his pillow.

"Absolutely not, never, no, thank you."

"Cool. Can I take this opportunity to say that I find it insulting that our guard is sleeping on the job?"

"Are you going to try to break out?" Sam asks him, already sounding like he's falling back asleep.

"Not tonight."

"Well then I'm going back to sleep. Let me know when you're breaking out."

"I don't want to ruin the surprise."

"Goodnight, guys," Ryan says. It sounds like a warning.

Either they listen or they're already asleep again. Doesn't matter, they don't respond.

"You okay?" Ryan whispers, his voice barely making a sound. It's more of a stirring of his breath near my face.

I shake my head, feeling humiliated and small. "Apparently not."

"What's wrong?"

I close my eyes hard, pinching them shut until I see bursts of light against the backs of my eyelids. A tear slips from the corner of my eye and runs down the side of my face. I cringe when it lands in my ear.

"I don't know. I think I had a dream."

Ryan settles on the floor beside the bed, his arm draped over my stomach. His hand is tracing slow circles on my forearm.

"A nightmare? Was it about the Risen?"

I chuckle darkly. "You mean the zombies?"

"Infected?"

"Undead?"

"Humanly challenged?"

I sigh, amazed that I'm actually smiling through my tears. I open my eyes to find him grinning at me.

"I think it was about my dad," I hear myself say.

I don't tell him that it was about my dad on Christmas day. That it was the same dream I always have and always ignore. The one about the tree, the door, the lights, the neighbor, the doll, the screams, the blood, the keys, the car, the days, days and days of being alone with nothing but my pink Hello Kitty bag full of snacks and treats left over from our road trip to grandma's house. That I never opened the door. That I peed in that car, in addition to other things. That I found my dad's iPod in the center console and I clung to it, silently sang the songs I knew were on it, but I never plugged it in, never listened to it because I knew if I made a sound or shone a single small light they'd find me. I don't tell him that they found me anyway. The Risen, the zombies, the infected, the undead, the sons of bitches that stole my light. My life.

I don't tell him, but I know when he looks at me that he understands it. He gets it because he's lived it. And because he sees me, like *really* sees me, and I want to hide from him but I don't. I don't because it's not so bad being seen. Not when it's by the right person.

"Joss, I'll sit here with you until—"

"Can I sleep down there with you?"

He's shocked. Me too, but I meant it. I mean it. I want it.

"Can I?" I press when he doesn't answer, only stares.

"Yeah, yeah, of course. Yeah," he stammers, making me smile faintly.

I grab my blanket and pillow then slide down onto the floor, onto his narrow mattress beneath me. When I lay down on my side facing the cage door, I feel him hesitate. I think he's scared. Scared of scaring me and I'm worried about it too but I want to know. I need to know if I can have him close like I think I want him to be and not freak out. Not break into a sweat or scream or run or punch him in the eye. I want to see if maybe it won't be bad at all because I think, I *hope*, it will actually be better.

And it is. When he lies down beside me, the length of his body running from my feet to my head, I feel safe. Secure. Like I'm open and vulnerable but it's okay because my back... my back is covered. It's against the wall. Against him. So when his arm hesitantly drapes over my side, I grab his hand in both of mine, pull it up against my chest and hug him to me hard. He's so close, so close. It's suffocating but I push past it because it's worth it and I want it. I want this. I want him. I want me when I'm with him, when I'm strong and I'm fighting and I'm trying for other people. When I'm alive and I'm hopeful and I'm not just surviving. I'm living, I'm laughing and I'm in lo—

***

"Wakey, wakey!"

I snap awake, my body jerking in every direction. My elbow hits a hard surface and I hear a shout behind me. I roll across the floor, look at where I'd been laying and see Ryan lying on his back with his hands clasped around his face.

"Jesus, Joss!" he cries.

I tentatively reach out to him, not sure what I plan to do to help. "Did I hit you?"

"Yes, you hit me. You elbowed me in the mouth. Who wakes up like that?"

I drop my hesitant hand and glare at him. "A girl who grew up in the wild, that's who. You shouldn't have been so close."

He stares at me in shock over the top of his hands still clutching his face. "You were holding onto me!"

"Is anything broken? Are you missing a tooth? If I knocked out a tooth, don't swallow it."

"You are the worst," he grumbles, sitting up.

"What do you want from me? I'm not a nurse and I'm not especially maternal."

When he drops his hands I see his lip is swelling on the right side. I got him good and it makes me feel awful inside. Sick in the pit of my stomach.

"An apology would be nice," he says.

"Ryan, I'm sorry I hit you beca—"

"Nope, that's enough," he interrupts, putting up his hand to stop me. "If you keep talking you're going to turn it around on me and the apology will mean nothing. Let's leave it at you're sorry you elbowed me in the face."

"Okay."

"Okay."

"I am sorry."

"I know."

"I didn't mean to hurt you."

"I know you didn't."

"I overreacted. I was wrong."

He grins. "Alright, Joss, don't hurt yourself."

"If you two are finished," Taylor calls from the doorway, "I'd like to get started so we can get it over with and I can go do something else."

"Like play Donkey Kong?" Sam asks, rubbing his

eyes.

Taylor glares down at him. "Were you sleeping?"

"No."

"Are you lying?"

"Yes."

"Perfect. They could have gotten out. Killed us all in our sleep."

"Nah, they're cool," Sam says, leaning back against the wall, completely unconcerned. He points to me. "That one is seriously damaged. No offense."

"None taken," I say through gritted teeth. He's not wrong, but still…

Sam points to Ryan. "He'd never go anywhere without her and she's here for something. Needs something. Neither of them is going anywhere. And him," he says, pointing at Trent. "I'm pretty sure he could have gotten out whether I was here or not, awake or asleep or dead. If he wants out, he'll get out."

"Your job was to watch them, not sleep."

"Are they still here? Then I did my job. I'm grabbing breakfast." Sam jumps up, heading for the door. He stops to point at me again. "Princess has requested eggs over easy, by the way."

With that Sam is gone and Taylor is shooting me daggers. I shrug.

"I mean, I wouldn't turn them down."

He shakes his head, leans into the hallway and shouts, "Bring in the med cart."

Ryan leans against the bars of our cage, standing beside me. Trent comes to stand beside him.

"What's the med cart?" Trent asks.

Taylor waves his hand. "Nothing major. We want to take some samples. Well, not *we*. The nurses and doc want samples. I want you gone."

Three more guards come into the room, one pushing a large metal cart that creaks and bumps over the uneven tiled floor of the hallways.

"Samples for what?"

"Information. We'll just take some measurements on you. Do a few tests, if you don't mind."

"And if we do?" Ryan asks brusquely, eyeing a large needle on the top of the cart.

Taylor shrugs. "Then you leave right now."

He sounds broken hearted about the idea.

"Just like that?" Ryan asks.

"Just like that."

I shake my head. I'm not leaving this place, not until I get to speak to the council or someone of some importance. Not until I've tried. They can bring in all the needles, knives and scary med equipment they want, I'm not being bullied out of this place.

"Do your tests," I tell Taylor defiantly, staring him in the eye to let him know I understand what he's trying to do. "We're not infected. We have nothing to hide."

He smirks. "Not that you know of. But the infection rate isn't what it used to be, not since *The Cure*," he says sarcastically. "Thanks to that little beauty of a failure, the last we checked incubation took over a week before a person fully turned, meaning you'll be locked in here for more than two. Are you prepared for that?"

It's nothing new. It's nothing we don't already know or haven't heard from him before, but the time frame is daunting. We can't be in here for two weeks. I've already been away from the Colony for too long as it is. People didn't have a lot of faith in me as a person to begin with. I doubt they've held out any hope I'll come back and that makes me so desperately sad inside. That I'm still trying but I know I've been written off because it's what I would have done. I would have given up and gone numb weeks ago.

"We don't want to move in," Ryan groans. "We just need to speak to someone. Someone who makes decisions for the group."

"How do you know you're not talking to him? How do you know I'm not the Grand Poobah? The king of the island?"

We all freeze when we hear a disembodied giggle from somewhere in the room. It's small and light, childish. Girly. I scan the room, trying to figure out where it's coming from. If maybe we heard it trickle down through a vent or if there's someone hiding somewhere in the room. Then one of the guards bends down, throws open the doors on the bottom half of the cart and there she is. A young girl with long dark hair and brilliant, shining blue eyes peering out at us. She blinks against the sudden light, then her eyes fix on us inside the cage, taking each of us in one by one. She can't be more than ten years old. Probably closer to nine. To eight.

"Beth, what the hell?" Taylor asks, exasperated.

She frowns, looking away. "I'm sorry, Taylor."

"What are you doing in there?"

"Playing hide and seek with daddy."

"Does he know he's playing this game with you?" Taylor asks suspiciously.

"No," she mumbles reluctantly.

"Cheater. Get out of here. You're not supposed to be in here, you know that. It's dangerous."

She goes to climb out of the cart but stumbles. One of the guards reaches down to help her out, to stand her up until she's there in front of us, vibrant with flushed cheeks, a clean face and hair and a daddy out there somewhere looking for her.

My throat begins to close up, making it hard to breathe.

"My mom lets me in here all the time," she whines.

"Yeah, when it's empty and it's just you and her. Seriously, sweetie, scram. Your dad will kill me—"

The doorway is filled with a tall man with brown hair, only one hand and brilliant blue eyes. Eyes the exact shade of the little girls.

It's her dad and my eyes are on fire.

"Taylor, have you seen Beth?" he asks.

Taylor silently points one stern finger at her face.

The man sighs with relief. "Come on," he tells her, his voice annoyed but affectionate. "Let's go."

She walks toward him reluctantly, taking her sweet time. "But I was going to help Taylor with the prisoners."

"You're eight years old, baby. Let's worry more about taking your bath and less about becoming a warden."

"Called it," I breathe, watching her go.

"What?" Ryan whispers.

I ignore him. I keep my eyes glued on the girl. On her dad.

"Hey, brat," Taylor calls after her, holding up a small, rustic doll that had been in the cart with her. It's ratty from use. Kind of an ugly thing. "Don't forget Little Miss, Little Miss Can't Be Wrong here."

The girl smiles brightly, giggling as she runs back to him to get her doll.

"Why do you call her that?"

"You don't know that song?"

She shakes her head, hugging her doll.

Taylor looks at the dad sadly. "Come on, man. You

aren't even raising her right."

"Blow me," the dad deadpans.

"What does that mean?" the little girl asks Taylor.

"It means don't repeat it. It also means Music Education in the rec room in an hour, you hear me?"

She smiles happily up at him. "Yes!"

"Alright, beat it."

She goes to leave with her dad, but she casts one last look over her shoulder at us. I see Trent, a tall blond blur in the corner of my watery eyes, waving to her. She lifts her hand to wave back but then her eyes catch on me and she hesitates. She stares at me, her sweet little girl face searing into my brain as she clutches that ugly, creepy doll that she loves so much. As she takes her dad's hand, his only hand, and walks out of the room.

"Joss, what's wrong?" Ryan asks me, his hand on my back.

I shake my head mutely, unable to speak without falling apart. I know my limits. I know when I've hit a wall and I just slammed headlong into a big one. But it's not the worst thing in the world. It's actually kind of... beautiful. Almost comforting. Because somewhere out there, despite everything that's happened, everything I've lost, there's a little eight year old girl with a daddy and a doll and a smile.

Chapter Sixteen

After three days, we've developed a routine. Wake up, fight with Taylor about leaving, eat our breakfast, give blood and tissue samples to whichever nurse or doctor they have on duty at the time, hang out in our cage until lunch, fight with Taylor about leaving again, eat, stare at each other, eat our dinner, fight with Taylor about leaving one last time for the day, then hang with Sam until it's lights out and we all go to sleep. We never talk about it, but I lay down next to Ryan every night, Trent snoozing just a few feet away. No one sleeps in the bed.

It's when one of the nurses, a thirty-something dark haired woman, is taking a sample from me that my injured arm finally comes back to haunt me. She's holding my hand, pulling on it lightly to keep me still as she looks for a vein. I'm not paying enough attention and she twists it, making me breathe in sharply.

Her eyes snap to mine. "What's wrong with your arm?"

"Nothing," I say tightly, waiting for the pain to subside. It's not terrible, just intense and surprising.

"She broke it," Trent tells the woman. He's watching us closely from his favorite corner. "Badly."

"It wasn't that bad."

"She threw up when she saw it. The bone was sti—

"

"Okay, it was bad!" I snap at him, looking at him hard. "But it's been healing."

The woman is gently probing my arm now, all the way up to the elbow. When I jerk and hiss again, she frowns.

"This needs to be casted," she tells me.

"What? Like a hard cast? Something I can't take off?"

"Exactly. Your arm needs to be immobilized, probably all the way through the elbow."

"Pass."

She raises her eyebrows. "It's not really a question."

"You're right, it's not because it's not happening," I tell her evenly. "I can't survive out there with a cast on my arm."

"You can't just leave it like this."

"Ryan splinted it, we can splint it again."

"I splinted it because it's all I could do," he calls from the bathroom, shouting through the shut door. "If I could have casted it, I would have."

I glare at the closed door. "Just do your business and don't worry about us out here, alright?"

"Do what you want, but you should let her cast it."

I turn to the nurse. "That's kind of creepy right? I don't know much, but I feel like talking to someone on the toilet is creepy."

She nods seriously. "It is, it's weird. But he's right. We need to do more than splint your arm."

I shake my head. "Not happening."

"Fine," she says with a sigh. "I'll splint it, then. But don't come crying to me when it heals wrong and hurts when it rains."

"Deal. Once I'm gone, I'll never come back."

"You just got here. You're that eager to leave us?" she asks, going back to her business of looking for a vein. She's taken hold of my other arm, leaving my injured one alone.

"Taylor is pretty clear that we're not wanted here."

The nurse smiles. "Yeah, he's not subtle. But it's not up to him. It's up to the council. If you can be of use to us here, they'll let you stay."

"We don't want to stay."

"What do you want, then?"

"Help."

She pauses, looking up at me. "Help with what?"

I swallow, not sure what to say exactly. Help fulfilling my promise? Help getting The Hive to agree to fight with us? Help freeing people from the Colony up north? Help taking down all of the Colonies? Help bringing down the Westbrook guy who's running the circus? I don't even know for sure. I'm not clear on how big of a part I'm meant to play in any of this. I haven't really stopped to think about it, not until right now. What is it that I want? Not what does everyone else want me to do or what do I need to get done to free myself from this burden, but what do I want out of all of this for my life?

"Help taking down the Colonies," I tell her adamantly, "ending the roundups and the kidnappings. Help making the resources the Colonies hoard and hide from us available to everyone willing to work and trade for them so the world isn't so damn cutthroat and horrifying."

She stares at me for a long time saying nothing. Not even moving. I can feel Trent staring at me too and I wonder if Ryan heard my rant. I try not to picture him right now, though.

"Those are some lofty goals," she tells me quietly. "You'll need a lot of help for that. Help we won't give you."

My heart plummets. "Why not?"

"Because as much as we hate the Colonies, we have something of a truce with them. They leave us alone, we leave them alone. Trust me, I'd like nothing more than to tear their buildings down on their heads with my bare hands, but I have a bigger picture to think about. Something bigger than my need for revenge."

"What did they do to you?"

Her eyes and mouth tighten at the corners. She's angry. "They tried to kill my husband. They said he was tainted. Dirty. Half dead like the monsters outside. Then they started saying the same thing about my daughter. They said I had laid with the damned and only evil could come from that. I put an arrow in a man's eye when he broke into my home to murder my family. To *cleanse* us. That was the last straw. We got out after that. We ran. We couldn't fight them, which is why I know you'll need a lot of help to do what you're planning. More help than The Hive can give you."

My blood runs cold. "Who said anything about The Hive?"

She looks at me hard. "They sent you here, didn't they?"

"How do you know that?" I whisper.

"Your boat has the name *U.S.S. Sweet Honey* written on the side of it with a small hornet painted on the rudder."

I close my eyes against what idiots we've been. How ill thought out and impulsive this entire thing has turned out to be. "I hate Marlow so much."

"Most people do," she agrees. "He's an idiot, though. Hornets don't even make honey. They eat insects, including each other."

"Like the cannibals."

"And the zombies, yeah. So you're part of The Hive?"

"No," I say firmly. "Absolutely not. We just went to them for help and they sent us here. They told us if we could get your people to join up, then they'd join us too. I know it's a lie, but we don't have a lot of options. We had to try."

"What's your plan?" the nurse asks, sitting down and leaning back, crossing her arms over her chest as she watches me.

I blink, surprised. "What?"

"Your plan. What was the pitch you gave to The Hive? Give it to me now. Sell it to me."

I glance at Trent who simply watches me as well, no indication of what he thinks I should say or do. So I figure what can it hurt?

I tell her everything. I start at the beginning with the day I was taken by the Colonists. I tell her about Vin, Nats and Breanne. About the Colony in the north in the MOHAI. About the crazy happy people running the show and the guard duty walking the wall, watching the interior to keep people in instead of keeping zombies out. I tell her about the kitchen crew, about the sewing room, about the maintenance room where Nats works. I tell her about the night I got jumped and she smiles when I tell her about the child's t-shirt and my failures as a seamstress. I tell her about the rebellion, the people desperately wanting out. Then I tell her about Caroline and her face changes. She's sad but she also looks understanding, the way Ryan looked at me when I told him. Like someone who knows. When I tell her about my jump and my fall, she nods in understanding as my broken bone suddenly makes sense. Then, when I'm done talking and Ryan is in the room with us again and no one is making a sound, she simply stares at me. I don't know what she's thinking. I definitely don't know if she believes me but as I look back at her, I really want her to.

"That's quite a story," she tells me.

But she doesn't.

She stands slowly, gathers her things and leaves the room without another word. I shake my head as I run my hands over my hair, pulling at it in frustration.

"No one is ever going to help us, are they? The Colonies will never stop. The roundups won't stop. The fear— dammit!"

"We could leave," Trent suggests. "Leave Seattle entirely. Live somewhere else where there are no Colonies."

"How do we know they aren't everywhere?" I ask him harshly.

"We don't know. Not until we look."

"No," I tell him, shaking my head again. "I can't just walk away. I can't leave them in there."

"We'll keep trying, Joss," Ryan tells me, but he sounds tired. Beat down like I feel. "We'll find a way to go back for them. I promise."

"Thanks," I mumble, but I don't believe him.

I don't think he does either.

***

"Still here, huh?" Taylor asks, flipping on the light.

I open my eyes slowly, making sure to take my time waking up. I've been working on that. On not freaking out and bashing Ryan in the face if I'm startled awake, something that happens more often than I'd like to admit. I'm like a skittish little deer and it sounds sweet, but not when you're the deer. Then it's just scary, humiliating and annoying. Ryan doesn't say anything about my new restrained demeanor, but I think every morning he wakes up without a fat lip or bloodied nose he counts it as a win. He could sleep somewhere else, somewhere away from me and my violent tendencies, but he never does. Some things, I think, are worth a little pain. I guess for him, sleeping beside me is one of them.

"Have we spoken to your council yet?" I mumble.

I open one eye to glare at him, not bothering to get up. It annoys Taylor when we sleep in so I do it as often as I can.

"Not yet, Princess."

"Then yep, still here. I'd be happy to go away if you'd let us talk to them."

"Not enjoying the accommodations?"

I sit up to stare at him, my face carefully blank. "It's a little Colonial for my taste."

Taylor shakes his head, a crooked grin forming on his face. "Watch what you say. I'll start to think you're one of them again."

I frown, surprised. "Meaning you don't think that now?"

"Meaning I have my doubts."

"Why is that?" Ryan asks.

Taylor folds his arms across his barrel chest, looking down at Ryan where he sits beside me. He glances over at Trent who stares back vacantly, his butt already perched in his favorite chair. When Taylor meets Ryan's eyes again, he looks far less annoyed than usual. Almost casual.

"You don't say grace."

"What does that have to do with anything?"

"A lot. The Colonists, the true to the bone followers, they're very religious. Devout."

"Overzealous," I mutter, thinking of Crenshaw.

Taylor nods. "Exactly that. They don't take a meal without saying grace or hit the sack without evening prayers. I'm not saying all religious people are Colonists just like I'm not saying all Colonists are religious. But I've seen you three dig into your food without washing your hands or thanking Jesus and to a genuine Colony follower, that wouldn't fly. So either you're just not one of the true followers, which makes it unlikely you'd be trusted to come in here to gather intel, or you're not with them at all."

"We're not with them at all," I insist.

Taylor shrugs. "Maybe you are or maybe you aren't, but Sam seems to think you're on the level so I'm inclined to give you the benefit of the doubt."

"You trust Sam's judgment that much?" Ryan asks dubiously.

"That kid is an excellent judge of character. Why do you think I have him in training with the guard? He'll have my job one day."

"Probably tomorrow," Sam mumbles from his cot, his face turned toward the wall.

"Chow is out," Taylor tells him.

Sam is up and out the door before any of us can say goodbye.

"If you don't believe we're spies," I say to Taylor, "then why won't you let us see your council yet?"

"Because that's not how it's done," he says simply.

"Never has been, never will be."

"We only want to talk to them. They could come here and—"

"It's not how it's done," Taylor repeats, this time more forcefully. "Look, here's the deal. The people on the council are important. President of the World important only with fewer sex scandals and racial discrimination. They absolutely will not be brought anywhere near you, any of you, until you've passed quarantine. Because I'm guarding you, I'm not allowed near any of them until the quarantine is over just as a precaution and that is messing up my game something awful."

"Your game?"

"He's boning one of the people on the council," Trent tells me.

I scrunch up my nose, grossed out by his phrasing. "I doubt he's 'boning' one of them."

"Trying to!" Taylor objects.

"Ugh," I groan.

"Get over it," he tells me, sitting down hard in a chair just outside our cage. It's the closest he's gotten to us without a tray of food since we got here. "The world has ended but life goes on and a big part of that for a man is a beautiful woman. Don't think for a second that your boy here likes sleeping curled up next to you because he's attracted to your soul and a morning punch in the mouth. He does it because you're soft and no matter how dirty you get, your hair smells like strawberries. It's a mystery of nature, but a fact nevertheless, one he'd like to get up close to and research further. More in depth, if you know what I mean."

"Speaking of messing up people's game," Ryan

growls from behind me.

I look back to see him shooting daggers at Taylor, his hand making a cutting motion across his neck.

Taylor chuckles. "Own it, kid. She needs to know and trust me, she won't mind. Badass as she wants to be, she's still a woman and even the toughest woman has times when she wants to feel like just that – a woman. Let me guess, Princess. Despite that rough exterior, you secretly like the fact that his hands are so much larger than yours. That they make yours feel delicate by comparison."

I'm calling it now – Taylor is a witch. A mind reading, secret spilling, smug SOB of the absolute highest order. He's also dead on. Ryan's broad shoulders, his large hands, the fact that he towers over me when he stands close; it all messes me up inside. It flips a switch I don't know how to turn off but maybe that's because I'm not trying hard enough. Or at all, really. I'm not trying because I like it. Because I want to swim around in it feeling fluid and free. Feeling like he's the wall between the rest of the world and me. Like I can lean on him. Count on him.

"Yeah," Taylor drawls, sounding satisfied as he watches me. "That's what I thought. Don't be embarrassed by it. Nothing makes a man feel more like a man than giving you that feeling and he makes you go all Go-Gurt inside, doesn't he?"

"What the hell is Go-Gurt?" I ask, evading the question.

"Sorry, that's probably before you're time. Sometimes I forget what younger people missed out on. Basically it's sweet flavored mush in a tube and that's you. Pure, sweet mush inside."

I want to tell him that he's an idiot and he's wrong,

but he's not. He's right and I'm pissed. I'm mad because I'm no longer a Jawbreaker. I'm more of a Gummy Bear or a friggin' Laffy Taffy. What am I supposed to do with that? How am I supposed to survive on the outside out in the wilds of Neverland with every Lost Boy and zombie in the world barreling down on me and I'm busted and cornered like Tinkerbell with a broken wing. They'll get me eventually, one of them will. I'll be put back in a cage that looks like a dream but you're never allowed to wake up. I'll go insane inside and eventually the mush will leak out and drown me in myself until I can't remember what it felt like to run. Until I'm one of those animals in Ryan's nightmare zoo, laying down for the last time and wondering where the world went.

"Joss," Ryan says, his voice cautious. It's the tone he takes when he knows I'm spooked. When I look like I feel – trapped.

"If you're done teaching sex ed, do you mind telling us how it started?" I ask hotly, desperate to change the subject but also wondering why we haven't asked them this yet.

Here's the thing. On the outside, out in the wild, no one knows. Even back when it was contained in Oregon, no one knew how the outbreak began. Or if they knew they sure as hell weren't telling. Reporters and wackos came up with wild theories about biological weapons, military experiments to create Super Soldiers that wouldn't die, some even said it came back to stem cell research gone wrong. Very few people believed it was just an illness that bloomed into being and wiped out the planet. Most were convinced someone was to blame. We just never found out who.

Taylor looks at me surprised. "How would I know?"

"Sam said you have military here," Ryan begins.

"Ex-military," Taylor clarifies.

"Either way, they were with the government when it went down. If anyone would know anything about it, it's them."

Taylor shakes his head. "They don't. They didn't then and they still don't."

Trent chuckles from his corner.

"What's funny?" I ask.

"Of course they don't know," he says coolly. "They were all soldiers, I imagine. No one very high up. They wouldn't have been given vital information like that."

"The government fell when you were just a kid," Taylor says incredulously. "How are you so jaded about it?"

"I read. And my father always hated the government."

"Trent grew up living off the grid," Ryan explains, probably because he knows Mr. Roboto never will. "He and his dad lived on a self-sufficient farm up in the mountains. His dad always expected a social collapse. It's why Trent is so... comfortable with the way the world is."

"He wasn't exactly prepped for zombies. That took him a little by surprise. He died in the first wave. I've never seen him so angry."

"Dying will do that to you," Taylor agrees.

"I'm sure he'd be proud of how far you've made it," Ryan tells him.

Trent shrugs. "He wasn't the sentimental type."

"Must be where you get your warmth and people skills," I tell him.

He grins. "That's from my mother's side."

"So no one knows how it started?" I ask in

amazement. "No one knows why we have to live like this? That's crap!"

"Would it matter?" Taylor asks. "What would it change?"

"Nothing," Ryan says darkly.

I can tell he's annoyed by this too. I know it wouldn't change anything but it doesn't stop me from wanting to understand. Honestly, I think I just want someone to blame. Some dipshit scientists or a government branch or all of it or no one. I don't know. I just want to know. I want a reason for why I've lived on the run and in hiding for the majority of my life. Why I'm jacked three ways from Sunday and can't even enjoy the little stupid things I want to enjoy. Little things like large hands and earnest eyes.

***

Two nights later, I'm called out as being a liar.

"You're lying, you have to be," Sam says, sitting back hard in his chair.

"I'm not!" I exclaim. "I'm dead serious, I don't get it."

Ryan groans, rubbing his hand over his eyes. "Joss, we've explained it so many times."

"Just write it down. Let me have a cheat sheet."

"So because you're bad at it, we should let you cheat?" Trent asks, shuffling the cards.

"No, that's not what I'm saying."

"That's exactly what you're saying," Ryan disagrees.

"I'm not cheating!"

"No," Sam says, "because if you were cheating, you'd be winning. I just think you're lying."

"I'm not!" I shout again, laughing. "I honestly do not get it."

"It's poker. It's not nuclear physics."

I roll my eyes. "I'm not stupid."

"No one said you were," Ryan tells me.

"We just said you're a liar," Sam adds.

"Ugh!" I shout, throwing poker chips at him.

"You're only making me richer," he laughs as he deftly catches every chip.

"Okay, explain the blind to me one more time. Then the river, I don't get the river."

"We're not explaining it again," Trent says.

"Then play without me, 'cause I don't understand half of what's happening here," I tell them, tossing my remaining few chips onto the center of the table.

Ryan shoves them back at me. "No way. You're in. Poker with only three people is pointless."

"We're basically playing with only three people now," Sam mutters under his breath.

Ryan and Trent chuckle, the traitorous bastards.

I'm about to lay into Sam, to insist that I'm in this game (or hand? Round? Cycle? I don't know) and I'll kick his ass this time, which I don't even know how to do but I *want* it, when the door flies open. It bangs hard against the wall, startling everyone. I jump up along with the boys, our legs knocking the table and sending chips and cards rolling and fluttering to the floor. Sam stands on the outside of the cage where he'd been playing poker with us through the bars, his surprised face fixed on the door.

There stands the brunette nurse, her normally calm face pinched in rage. She stalks toward us in the cage, her eyes fixed hard on me. I nearly cower under that stare but I've lived too long in the wild to flinch so easily. When she whips out a gun, though, something I haven't seen in years, I blink rapidly. I can't believe my eyes. I can't believe she still has one and I want to doubt she has any bullets left for it, but the look on her face tells me that she absolutely, positively does. And one of them has my name on it.

"No, Ali, what are you doing?" Sam exclaims, coming to stand beside her.

She cast him a quick look that tells him to back off. He does slowly, his hands raised.

"She's cool, I swear," Sam tells her. His voice is rising in pitch with his nerves. "She's not a zombie."

Feet are rushing around the house. I hear the front door fly open, boots pounding on the tile floor of the hall and entryway. People are running upstairs above us. Someone is shouting but it's too muffled to understand.

The brunette, Ali, looks at me. Her hand holding the gun never wavers.

"You're going to answer my questions and then you're going to die so you may as well be honest, do you understand me?"

"Huckleberry!" Sam cries.

Ryan, Trent and I all stare at him, confused as hell.

"Huckleberry, Ali! I swear it! Don't do this!"

"Calm down, Sam," she tells him evenly, never looking away from me. "I'm crystal clear. I know what's what and these three are spies."

"What?" I exclaim, shocked. "No, no we're not. I promise."

"Lies. You're spies for the Colonists, which leads me to my first question. What were you supposed to accomplish once you were inside?"

I shake my head, my breath coming hard in short, painful gasps. "I don't know what you're talking about.

We're not working with the Colonists."

She cocks the gun. Ryan steps closer to me but one look from Ali sends him right back where he was. She focuses her eyes on me again.

"We haven't had strangers on this island in years. Then suddenly you three show up in a Hive boat with insider knowledge about the Colonies. Now, just days later, Colony ships are creeping through the Sound heading our way in the dead of night, obviously planning an ambush. So I'll ask you again, what were you meant to accomplish while you were here? What did they send you to do? Were you supposed to disable our power supply somehow? What were you planning?"

"All we wanted," Ryan says calmly, trying to draw her attention away from me, "was to speak to someone in your council about getting help freeing our friends from a Colony. That's all. Trent and I, we're members of a gang on the outside but it's not The Hive. It's also too small to be of any help. So we went to The Hive and they sent us to you. That's the entire truth."

Ali shakes her head, her mouth forming a perfect line on her face. It makes me sweat down to my toes.

"Try again," she whispers darkly.

"Lower the gun and talk to us about this," Ryan insists firmly.

"No time for that. The ships are almost here and if they manage to overtake this island, I'm not about to leave you alive. So I'll ask one more time, what were you meant to do here?"

"We were meant to find Heaven," I tell her softly, thinking of Crenshaw. I'm so used to not mentioning him, never talking about him to keep him safe, that I suddenly realize I never mentioned him in my story to her. I only ever told Taylor about him and the name didn't ring a bell so I never brought it up to Ali. That seems infinitely stupid to me now. It's amazing what clarity a gun to the face can bring.

"See, now we're getting somewhere. God, Heaven and divine retribution, that's all Colony talk."

"No, it's Crenshaw. Except he called it Elysium."

My blood screams in my body when she blinks. His name means something to her.

"Crenshaw is the one who told us about you originally," I continue, hoping to hit home again with his name. "He said we never should ask The Hive for anything. That they were liars and traitors and he was right. I should have listened to him. He showed us a map, told us he helped you plant a garden here and that he had an open invitation to join whenever he wanted but he won't because he's waiting."

Ali takes a deep breath. Her fingers flex slightly on the handle of the gun.

"What is he waiting for?" she asks, her tone giving nothing away.

"His daughter," Ryan says softly. "The Hive has his daughter and he'll never leave her."

Her eyes dart from me to Ryan, to Trent and back again. Finally, she lowers the gun.

"What's your name?" she asks me.

"Joss."

She shakes her head minutely. "No, what's your name?"

I frown, suddenly unsure. "Jocelyn."

Whatever softness was building in her leaks away. The gun is back in my face in an instant.

"Wrong answer."

Gun = clarity.

"Athena!" I cry, finally understanding. "He calls

me Athena. He said Joss was too mousy for—"

"A warrior like you," Ali finishes for me, the gun lowering again.

I nod quickly, though it's more like shaking. I gesture to Ryan. "That's Helios."

Ali looks to Trent who shrugs, unconcerned.

"We're not that close," he admits.

Ali stares at each of us in turn. No one else moves. We stand statue still, all very aware of the gun hanging heavy and dark at her side. She stares at me the longest, her face carefully blank. Then suddenly she nods curtly as though coming to an agreement with me, an agreement I know nothing about.

"Sam," she says, turning to face him, her entire demeanor changing. She suddenly seems tired. Her movements are slower. Sluggish. "Let them out. I'm not the only one who will be coming for them, I just got here first. Once they're out, take them to their boat at the old pier. It's tied up there."

"You're letting us leave?" Ryan asks hopefully. "Alive?"

Ali looks at him, a sad smile on her lips. "Any friend of Crenshaw's..."

She turns to leave as Sam is unlocking our door. Maybe it's foolish, maybe it's tempting fate, but I call out to her.

"Thank you."

She pauses in the doorway, her face cut in half by the light in the room and the shadow beyond it.

"Don't thank me yet. I doubt you'll make it past the buoys."

"What's the deal with the buoys?" Ryan asks.

She ignores him. Her eyes are fastened on mine.

"If you see Crenshaw again," she says, her voice

soft and affectionate, "tell him Persephone sends her love."

Chapter Seventeen

When she's gone, Sam swings the door to the cage open. Not waiting for us to get out, he runs across the room to a large cabinet and unlocks it quickly. Inside are our weapons. When I take hold of my ASP in my shaking hand, my brain and body still coming down from the gun in my face, I feel better. Less like wetting myself and more like kicking a little ass. Crushing skulls and forgetting names.

"We'll go out the back way," Sam says, checking to see if the hall is clear.

It sounds like most of the people have moved outside. There's the sound of shouting wafting in through the door that's been left open and I can see lights scattering around the huge front lawn. There are vehicles, flashlights and torches but mostly there's bodies. Lots and lots of moving, running, frantic bodies, none of which I want to come in contact with right now.

When the house is silent he runs us out of the library, down a long corridor that leads to the kitchen and out the back door. When we hit the backyard, I'm momentarily floored by the fact that there's a swing set with a slide and sandbox out here. The little girl with the eyes and the doll must live here permanently. I can see her here, laughing and running with her dad nearby, her mom in the kitchen. Both of them with a gun on their hip and a knife in their shoe.

Sam sprints us over the dark lawn toward the back of the property. There are other people out here running around, but they're farther down on the other side of the house. No one pays us any mind. Eventually we reach bushes that we dive straight into. The branches claw at our clothes trying to hold us back. I hear a rip as I run through them and I know yet another coat of mine is torn. I'm suddenly wishing I'd paid more attention in sewing class.

"Over here," Sam calls quietly.

I don't know why he's bothering with stealth. The world has gone insane around us. People are shouting, horns are blaring, lights flash in every direction.

He leads us up to the fence, then without looking back to see if we're following, climbs it like a crazed monkey. He's up and over in only a few seconds, taking any thoughts I may have had about these people possibly going soft right over with him. I glance at the boys, feeling like it was a challenge. One I'm not sure we can rise to but I'm sure as hell gonna try.

I take a couple of steps back, then launch myself at the fence. I tune it all out – the noises, the fear, the stress of the moment, all of it. I focus only on getting over the fence and to the other side without tearing my clothes any more than I already have and without landing on my face on the other side. I'm grinning ear to ear when I land firmly on my feet beside Sam, the water from the Sound lapping gently on the shore not far behind us.

Ryan and Trent clear the fence, though I'm pleased to see Trent struggle a little bit. Mr. Roboto isn't perfectly agile. It's good to know.

Once we're all together again, Sam runs us to the

west along the shore. It's not long before I spot it – our ill-fated, ill painted Hive boat. I wish they'd burned it. I'm with Ryan on this one; Marlow isn't getting that thing back in one piece.

"There it is," Sam breathes, halting not far from the pier. "Take it and go. Get clear of the buoys as quick as you can, but steer clear of the Colony ships too."

"What the hell are the buoys for?" Ryan asks, sounding annoyed that he's yet to get an answer on that question.

Then he gets one. Just as I'm pointing to the boats cutting through the water and closing in fast, the night explodes in light and sound. It comes from behind us inside the island, then it cuts across the sky like a comet ripping through the night. It's huge, angry and it's on fire. It lands near one of the boats, missing it by mere feet. Then another one launches not far behind it. This one arcs a little higher, crossing the water a little bit farther and then it connects solidly with the Colony boat. The boat erupts in flames. I hear screams coming across the water that's growing choppier by the minute. They won't put it out. Whatever that ball was made of, it exploded and it carried flames with every inch of it. The boat is now a floating funeral pyre.

"That's what they're for," Sam tells him. "Now go and stay away—"

"From the buoys, yeah. Got it," Ryan agrees. He puts out his hand to Sam who takes it and pulls him into a quick hug, both of them slapping the other on the back twice hard. "Thanks, man. Take care."

"Yeah, you too. Good luck out there."

When Sam is gone, running back up the shore toward his people shouting and preparing to fire another blazing ball of ugly, we run the short distance to the old, broke down pier.

"So, I don't get it. What are the buoys exactly?" I ask, climbing in.

Ryan helps Trent untie us then starts hoisting a sail. "They're distance markers. They let the people firing know how far out the boats are so they shoot more accurately."

"What are they shooting? Cannons?"

"Trebuchet," Trent says, taking the rudder. We slowly begin moving across the water, his eyes watching the buoys and boats carefully. There are a lot of them in the way, in between us and open water. Safety. This is going to be tricky. "It's like a catapult. It has a long sling arm with weight on the other end. When the weight drops, it shoots the arm up which drags the sling and flings whatever weapon you loaded in it toward your target."

"From the looks of it," Ryan says eyeing the burning boat, "they're using burning oil or tar."

"Maybe they figured out the secret to Greek Fire," Trent whispers reverently.

I look at him in surprise. "What's Greek Fire?"

He shrugs. "No one knows what it was exactly, but it burned on water. Scientists tried for ages to figure it out but they could never recreate it. Maybe returning to medieval methods of warfare has made people more resourceful than a curious scientist in a lab coat."

"Can't be it," Ryan says, sounding disappointed. "It's going out when it hits the water."

"Damn," Trent mutters.

"Okay, but whatever it is," I say, pulling them out of their fanboy funk, "we need to avoid it. I don't think the people operating the treb… the things are going to be picky about hitting us."

"Trebuchet, and you're right," Ryan agrees. "Should we drop the sail? Float inconspicuous?"

"No," Trent tells him, sitting up straighter. "Because we've just been spotted. We need to get out of here."

One of the Colony boats is closing in on us, probably mistaking us for a strike from the Vashons. It's large and long, what used to be used to ferry people back and forth between the island and different parts of the bay, I think. It's hulking, rusting hull is barreling down on us, the water breaking noisily in an angry white froth ahead of it. Trent guides us in the opposite direction which also happens to be straight into the fight. Right into the line of fire. There are tons of ships and buoys around us, every one of them a big red flag full of nope.

More fireballs rain from the sky. I can hear it coming and I duck, although what good could it really do. The missile hits the bow of the ship chasing us. It erupts in flames that I can feel as well as hear. More shouts, much louder now that they're closer, rip through the night. The cold air superheated on one side of me while the other side is covered in goose bumps.

"Get us out of here, Trent!" Ryan cries, scanning the boats around us. No one else is taking notice of us.

"Yeah, cause I wasn't already trying."

We slip between two large ships, more ferries I think, and I look up, worried they'll drop buckets of burning oil on us the way the Vashons are firing on them. Luckily, we continue to be ignored. They have bigger problems than us. The Vashons are seriously destroying them. As far as I can tell, there's only one ship not engulfed in flames. The one on our right that's passing by us, heading for a green buoy.

"Guys, what was the first buoy we saw? Was it

green? Was that the farthest out?" I ask breathlessly, daring to hope we're in the clear.

"No, it was pink, then—"

The boat beside us explodes in flames that spill over the sides, scorching hot in the cold water around us. I duck down, covering my head with my hands and I feel Ryan throw himself on top of me. There's screaming and shouting from above us, Ryan shouting beside my head to Trent.

"The sail! The sail!"

"I can't put it out!"

"Trent, duck!"

The boat rocks violently to one side. Ryan and I bang against the hull, water pouring in and drenching my pants. Then the ship tilts even farther, heat rising on what little exposed flesh I have, then it's dark, silent and icy cold as death. The boat has capsized. We're in the water.

I can't feel Ryan anywhere near me so I kick to the surface, desperate to find him. When I break the water, I'm alone. The boat is upside down, its algae stained hull exposed to the air and fire and stars. For a brief moment as the flames flare up on the boat beside me, I can see the small hornet drawn on the rudder. The one Ali told us about.

"Double crossing Captain Hook," I growl.

I will kill that man if given the chance.

"Ryan!" I shout, spinning around in the water. "Ryan! Trent!"

"Over here," Trent calls quietly.

I thrash to the left, spotting him a ways off in the shadows. He's nothing but a head in the water but he's floating and breathing so I'm happy.

"You okay?" I ask him, swimming toward him. My

arm aches with the effort but it's not as bad as it could be. I'm relieved it's at least splinted again.

"Been better. I hit my head."

"How hard?"

"Hard. Too hard. There are two of you."

"Great," I grumble, coming to a stop beside him. I reach up and touch the back of his head. My hand comes away wet, of course, but I can tell from the thickness and warmth of it that it's blood. "Are you okay to swim?"

"Yeah, I'll be fine. Where's your boy?"

"I don't know," I tell him, panic welling up inside of me. "He was with me when we went in, but I can't see him. Can you?"

Trent shakes his head, winces. "I can't see much of anything besides stars."

"Ryan!" I shout. "Ryan!"

"Wait, shut up."

I scowl at Trent. "You shut up."

"No, seriously, shut up. Do you hear that?"

All I hear is the sound of chaos all around us and blood in my ears as my heart races out of control. I've never been so scared in all my life and it's all his fault. All because of Ryan. Because of caring.

"Hear what?" I ask impatiently.

"Thumping. From the boat hull."

I dive toward the boat, pressing my hands and ear to the slimy surface. I can hear it. A frantic pounding from inside. I sink under the water, reaching for the lip of the hull so I can slip under and up inside. When I make it, I break the surface looking around and calling his name.

"Ryan?"

A hand grabs onto my injured arm, yanking it hard

and pulling me under the water. I go to cry out in pain and surprise when water fills my mouth. My lungs. The hand doesn't let go. It pulls me under and to the side. I force my eyes open in the water but all I see is darkness. Then there he is, the ghostly white outline of Ryan's face. His eyes are bulging wide with terror and desperation. He's drowning.

I can see his coat hooked on something on the hull. I grab onto it, tugging as hard as I can but I can't get him free. He's being held sideways against the hull, his booted foot the only thing out of the water. It's what was banging on the boat.

He grips my hand harder. I open my mouth involuntarily, gurgling in pain. Then I get an idea. I jerk free of him, sending agony up into my shoulder, and I break the surface. Taking in a deep gulp of air, I dive under again until I'm level with him. Then I grab his face in both my hands, press my mouth to his and I breath into him. I give him everything I have in my lungs, every ounce of life I'm holding onto. Then I break for the surface again.

"Trent!" I scream. "Trent, help me!"

I take two steady breaths, make sure I'm calm and breathing even, then I take a large gulp and dive under again to give it all to Ryan. When I break the surface for more air, to buy more seconds of Ryan's life, I see Trent come up inside the hull.

"You have to help me," I say quickly, speaking faster than I've ever spoken in my life. "Ryan is trapped. I can't get him loose and he's going to die. I'm giving him air but he's stuck."

Trent nods quickly then dives under the water without a word. I take another large breath and dive under after him. While Trent works to free Ryan, I press my mouth to his again. I do this several more times, more times than I can count. Trent has to come to the surface twice for more air, but he keeps diving back down. He doesn't quit. I'm starting to feel dizzy when I go down again and press my mouth to Ryan's. I barely notice that he doesn't grab onto me. But then it strikes me that he doesn't respond at all and when I pull away, I watch in horror as bubbles of air escape his lips, passing over his closed eyes.

"Ryan!" I shout, knowing he can't hear me and that I'm wasting my own air. But I can't hold it in.

Finally Trent has him free and his body floats upward. We both grab onto him and yank him toward the surface, kicking as hard as we can as we pull his dead weight with us.

When we have our heads above water in the hull, Trent turns Ryan around in his arms. He puts Ryan's back to his front and wraps his arms around him like he's giving him a weird hug. Then they both sink slightly as Trent puts all his strength into squeezing hard and fast on Ryan's stomach. Ryan lurches forward, his face falling in the water. I reach out to steady them, to try to help Trent keep him afloat.

"What are you doing?" I ask him, my voice shaking.

"I'm getting the water out of his lungs," Trent grunts, then he jerks on Ryan again. Nothing. Trent's calm face is pinched in concentration and anxiety. "Come on, come on."

I hold onto Ryan's face with both my hands as I tread water with my feet. I carefully brush his hair out of his closed eyes, willing them to open. To be brown and beautiful and alive.

"Come on," I whisper, chanting with Trent. The

sound of our low voices fills the hull of the boat, rebounding off the water and echoing around us. "Come on, Ryan. Please."

Trent sinks again, jerks hard on Ryan and I get a face full of water when Ryan suddenly spurts and sputters. He chokes violently for several seconds then vomits into the darkness. I don't even care. He's fighting for breath, breathing in and out, no matter how raggedly, and I start crying my eyes out when his own eyes flutter open and he looks at me.

"Ryan," I breathe, my voice coated in tears.

He coughs, more water spurting out of his mouth violently. He reaches out blindly to grab onto the hull and hold himself up but his hands slip off the smooth sides. Trent and I hold onto him tightly, both of us giving up our arms to keep him afloat as he tries to get his bearings.

He takes several ragged breaths before saying hoarsely, "I can't swim."

I laugh despite my tears, taking his face in my hands again and staring into his open eyes. At his mouth pulling in air and blowing it out forcefully. His pulse throbbing at his throat, beating with his heart, moving through my veins.

Chapter Eighteen

Ryan isn't kidding. He seriously can't swim.

That's going to be a problem. It's one we solve by finding a piece of floating debris, a task that is disturbingly easy with almost all of the Colony boats blown up and burning in the water. A couple are heading for the hills, back up the Sound as fast as their hobbled ships can carry them, but most of the boats are burned beyond salvage. It didn't take long. The Vashons laid their armada to waste in no time. Almost like they had planned for years for such an attack.

As we swim/paddle toward the opposite shore, I wonder what this night means for the Vashons 'uneasy treaty' with the Colonists.

I also wonder what provoked the Colonists to suddenly attack.

When we make it to shore all three of us lay on the ground breathing heavily and shivering. The water was cold, but being out in the open now while wet feels even colder. We need to make camp somewhere nearby soon and start a fire or we'll all get pneumonia and die.

"We need to get moving," I groan, sitting up. I feel weighed down by exhaustion and wet clothes.

When I look over at the boys I find both of their eyes closed.

"Hey!" I shout, clapping my hands hard. They both startle, both of their eyes shooting open. "No sleeping, not here. Especially you, Trent. The last thing we need is you dying in your sleep."

He sits up slowly. "I don't have a concussion."

"Good news. Unless you want hypothermia, it's time to move."

"It's not cold enough for that," Ryan protests. He's still lying down.

I lean over him, my face near his and his my hair hanging out him. "It's cold enough to get sick. Get your ass up."

He reaches up to run his hand over my cheek, back into my hair. "You saved my life."

"Don't get mushy on me. Get up."

He pulls my face down farther and kisses me soundly on the mouth. I don't fight it because it's warm, it's him and he's alive. I can't stop to think about how happy I am that he didn't die out there. I can't think about what would happen to me if I lost him. Where my heartbeats would go without his to follow.

I pull away. "Move. Now."

"So bossy," he grumbles, but he gets up.

We've come ashore in an old industrial area. This is good and bad. Good because it's probably abandoned. Bad because there won't be much to make a fire with and we absolutely have to have a fire.

"Where do you think we are?" I ask quietly as we slowly make our way through the rusted rubble.

"Judging by the light in that direction," Trent says, pointing to our left, "I'd say we're just south of the stadiums."

"Perfect. So we have to get by the Colonies to get home."

"We have to go through the valley," Ryan says.

"The what?"

"On Crenshaw's map. Remember the valley between the stadiums and the dark shadowy area. He said the space between was the Valley of the Shadow of Death."

"And the black area was the portal to Hell," I say, remembering it suddenly.

Ryan cocks an eyebrow at me. "He told us not to go there."

"He also told us not to go to The Hive."

"My point exactly."

"We can't avoid it," I protest, feeling frustrated.

Trent stops short suddenly, looking around with his wicked hawk eyes. "We'll make camp here."

"Okay, why here?"

"Because over there," he says, pointing ahead and to the left of us, "are the Colonies, just two blocks away. And over there," he points to our right, "another two blocks away are the cannibals."

"Are you kidding me?" I hiss, immediately going tense. "We're near the cannibals? How do you know that?"

He frowns at me like I'm stupid. "Because I've seen them."

"Of course you have. We can't stay here."

"We can't go back either and we definitely don't want to go any farther forward. Not at night."

"Why not at night? The Colonists won't be able to see us as well."

"I'm not worried about the Colonists. At night, you have to worry about the cannibals. They're very territorial, they live underground and they only come out at night. Right now, they can see better than I can.

A lot better."

"Oh man," I moan, wrapping my arms around myself. "So right now not only do we have to worry about zombies and pneumonia, we have to worry about being kidnapped by Colonists and being eaten alive by cannibals?"

"There are also a lot of mosquitos this close to the water."

"Oh my God," I mutter.

"We'll be alright," Ryan tells me. "Let's start a fire and—"

"A fire? Are you crazy? It'll call them all right to us."

Ryan shakes his head. "We have to have a fire, Joss. We need to dry off, to warm up. It can't be helped."

"We'll go over there inside that shack," Trent says, pointing to an old security building at the entrance of the parking lot we're standing in. "We'll bust out the windows if they're not already gone to let the smoke out, but the building should block most of the light from the fire."

"Fine," I say reluctantly, knowing they're right. "But when we die, I want you both to remember I told you so."

"Noted," Ryan agrees.

Luckily the shack is a complete mess. Complete mess means things to burn. Things that have been inside and kept from most of the elements, most importantly moisture. Only one window is broken. Trent wastes no time breaking two more while Ryan and I get to work building our fire inside an old metal trash can. It's easier than you'd think, but then again, we've had practice. Lots and lots of practice.

Once it's burning in the center of the room, we

huddle around it. I drape my torn, wet coat over a chair to let it dry faster. I'm shivering from head to toe so when Ryan wraps his arm around me and pulls me in close to his body, I don't fight it. I tense and my breathing gets tight, but I try to hide it. I don't want to hate this. I want to like it, and a big part of me really, really does but a little part of me is still afraid. Maybe it always will be.

"Why didn't they search us for weapons when we went to see Marlow?" I ask, suddenly remembering I had meant to ask Ryan before.

He nods thoughtfully. "I wondered that too. Every time I've been in to see him, my weapons were taken."

"Did they just forget?"

Ryan chuckles. "You don't forget something like that. Not working for Marlow."

"Not if you want to live," Trent agrees.

"So I'm not crazy? It was weird."

"Yeah, it was."

"He's going to be mad about his boat."

"No, he won't be, not really, but he'll act mad," Ryan says darkly. "He'll use it as a way to get something from us."

"He never meant for us to make it back alive did he?"

"I don't know."

"Oh come on. He sent us there in the *U.S.S. Sold You Out*. It couldn't have been more obvious we were associated with The Hive and the Vashons obviously don't like them."

"Yeah, but why?" Ryan insists. "Why send us there to have them kill us? I think he wanted to see if it would work."

"He wanted us to draw them out," Trent says.

"Probably take a few of their people prisoner to barter for something."

"What though? Land? Turnips?" I ask.

"Probably guns."

I shiver involuntarily as I remember the black barrel of Ali's gun pointed at my face.

"Do you think that gun was loaded?" I ask quietly.

"It was," Ryan replies softly, his grip on my upper arm tightening.

I nod, knowing he's right. I knew it when I looked at her face. She was ready, willing and fully able to kill me on the spot. But I don't hate her for it. I don't blame her at all. She didn't do it to protect her soft bed or a fluffy pillow. It wasn't for the sake of central air or a good hot meal at the end of the day. It was for her family. For her daughter and her husband. For the people she loves.

Sitting beside this fire with Ryan's arm around my shoulder, I can easily understand that.

"So Marlow will be mad when we get back that we lost his boat and didn't bring him his bounty," I surmise, "and Crenshaw will be mad that we went to The Hive first and pissed off the Vashons. The Vashons are mad at us, probably all of them want us dead because they think we brought the Colonies to their door in an ambush."

"By now word has gotten out about what Trent and I have been up to, my fight in The Hive not sanctioned by the Hyperion, going behind the backs of our brothers. We'll be thrown out of the gang."

"Will they hurt you?" I ask.

Trent grins, his face lit in a macabre mask by the firelight. "They're welcome to try."

"I'm so sorry," I whisper, feeling like an asshole. I

drug them into this and now their lives are ruined. "You're both obviously welcome to come live with me in the loft."

"Don't worry about it, we'll figure something out," Ryan tells me, sounding unconcerned. It's both a relief and a little bit painful that he doesn't take me up on the offer.

"You two should get some sleep," Trent says. "I'll stay up and take first watch."

"Are you sure, man?"

"Yeah, I got it. I'm not tired."

"Good, cause I'm exhausted. Wake me up in a couple hours. I'll take next shift."

"You got it."

"I'm not tired," I tell them, staring into the fire. "I'll stay up too."

Ryan frowns at me. "Are you sure?"

I smile weakly, nodding. "Yeah, I'm sure. I need to relax a little. Come down from what's happened tonight. You sleep, though. You have to be tired from…"

He grins. "Nearly dying."

My smile fades. "Don't do that again."

"I don't plan on it."

"Good."

"Thanks, by the way. To both of you." He looks at Trent, his mouth going tight. "I'd be dead if it weren't for you guys."

Trent shakes his head. "We didn't do anything you wouldn't have done for us. It's nothing special. Go to sleep."

Ryan nods silently before sprawling out beside me. He's between me and the door again, a position I'm beginning to think he'll always take. It speaks volumes and I'm finally beginning to understand the language it's written in. I'm not fluent yet, but I'm getting the gist of it.

It's not long before Ryan is snoring away. I look across the fire at Trent, giving him a small smile.

"So," I say softly, "how much trouble are you guys going to be in really?"

Trent watches me for a second, his face blank. Finally, he says, "A lot."

I nod, hating it but knowing it's true. I'm glad he's willing to be real with me about it. "What can I do?"

"Nothing. What's done is done."

"I really am sorry. I didn't mean to do this to you both."

"It'll be worse for Ryan than for me. They were like a family to him. I was only there because of Ryan and Kevin."

"How did you all end up together?"

He smirks. "How do any of us end up together?"

"You don't want to talk about it."

"Not any more than you do. Don't feel bad about it, though."

"Which part?" I chuckle unhappily.

"Any of it. I don't mind and Ryan wouldn't have done things any differently. If you needed his help, he was going to give it."

I frown, shaking my head slightly. I'm too embarrassed to look him in the eyes anymore.

"I can't understand that."

"Are you sure?"

I shake my head again.

"How many times did you go back under the water for him? How many breathes did you give up? How many would you have given?"

All of them. Every last one of them. I never would

have stopped.

I feel dizzy. Disoriented. I take several deep breathes, trying to get my bearings. Trying to find my center, my numb, but it's been gone too long. I can't get it back. I want to retreat into myself and hide from everything, all of it that's not working and the things that are working too well, but I can't. I'm in the thick of it now. I'm living life surrounded by so many more things than I realized were out there, so many more dangers than I ever dreamed of. There's so much more to fear than just the Risen, the Colonists and the gangs. There's so much more to gain. To lose.

I look up at Trent, about to ask him to tell me the story of how he met up with Ryan and Kevin, even if it means I have to tell my own in return. I'm ready for that. I think I can do it. I at least want to try. But the look on his face freezes my breath in my throat.

"What is it?" I whisper, knowing whatever it is, it isn't good.

Trent stares at me patiently, his weird, light eyes looking white in the firelight.

"We aren't walking out of here in the morning," he replies, his deep voice vibrating through my bones.

I swallow hard. "Why not?"

"Because they're coming."

My vision goes funny, fuzzy. I'm having trouble breathing. "No one is coming. No one knows we—"

"I can hear them," he interrupts me, his voice hushed and calm. "They're not even trying to hide themselves. They want us to know."

"Why?" I whisper, my eyes glued on his. My ears straining to hear the evil that speaks only to him.

"Because," he says, his voice dipping lower. I can hear it then, behind his words. Footsteps. Slow, unhurried. Patient. "They want us to run."

I bite my lip until I taste blood, willing myself not to cry out. Not to jump up and run, to leave them both behind.

"Who?"

I hear the screech of metal over the pavement. It's not far off. A blade being drug over the ground. A warning. A promise.

"You know who."

I nod hard.

"The cannibals."

Chapter Nineteen

Vashon Island

Ali stands at the edge of the water, separated from the rest of the crowd. They're shouting with excitement because they think they've won. But she knows this enemy better than most. Not all of them were there at the start. Not all of them watched the evil grow, seeding from one man, one idea, to ten then twenty then a hundred. Thousands. Tonight, this victory, it's only the beginning of a war and that cold realization makes her understand that the life they've lived for the last ten years has been on borrowed time. This was always going to happen. It would always come to this.

This was always how it was going to end.

"They're on the run," Jordan tells her, coming to stand behind her.

She shakes her head. "Tonight they are, but tomorrow…"

"I know."

And he does. He was there with her at the start. He saw it all.

"Are you hiding?" he asks quietly.

Ali sighs. "I swore I never would again."

"They're going to come looking for you soon. Once they realize the prisoners are gone."

"I know."

"Are you sure about them?"

She chuckles darkly. "As sure as I am about anything."

"Sam agrees with you."

"That is remarkably comforting."

"Taylor is going to side with you too. He doesn't believe they were Colony spies. He thinks they were idiots, but not spies."

"They're just young," she says, sounding sad and tired, "and desperate."

Jordan wraps his arms around her from behind, resting his chin on the top of her head of long, dark hair. She takes his hand in hers.

"I can remember being that desperate," he mumbles.

"Me too. It's part of why I let them go."

"What was the other part?"

She smiles. "They knew Crenshaw."

He chuckles behind her, shaking her body with the movement. "Oh, Persephone. You have such a soft spot."

"You're just jealous he never gave you a name."

"I'm hurt he named you after a woman married to the king of Hell. What does that say about me?"

"It says you're strong. Strong enough to endure."

"Hmm," he murmurs thoughtfully, not buying it.

"Do you think they made it?" she asks.

"I don't know. Maybe, if they were lucky."

"I lost sight of them once most of the ships were burning."

"It's a beautiful night for it."

She grins. "For what exactly?"

When he speaks, she can hear the familiar sound of

a smile in his voice. "For smiting your enemies."

"You know what's sad?"

"Soy milk."

She rolls her eyes. "Jordan."

"It's not real milk, Ali. It's imposter crap and I won't drink it. I won't drink a lie."

"Jordan."

"Tell me. What's sadder than soy milk?"

"This isn't the first time I've stood in the dark with you watching the world burn."

He pauses, going serious. "It's not even the second time."

"More like fifth."

"Sixth, I think."

She sighs heavily, turning to look up at him with watery eyes. "When will it end? When will Beth be safe?"

"I don't know," he says softly, shaking his head. He lifts his hand to press it against her cheek. To wipe a stray tear away. "Probably never. Not unless—"

"Unless?"

His eyes drift past her to the burning boats. To the fire on the water. To the shore on the other side swarming with zombies, Colonists and gangs. To the world they outnumber. A world they could easily overrun, if only given the right incentive. The right reasons. The right time.

"Unless we end it."

Watch for the next book in the
Survival Series, *Tearing Down the Wall*.
Coming Summer 2014!

Keep reading for the first chapter from
Tracey Ward's highly rated
sci-fi novel, *Sleepless*.
Available now!

Prologue

Nick

The first time I saw her, I was dead.

I was rolling down the river with two coins for the Ferryman, heading out onto the infinite, black sea. Worst of all, I was going without a fight.

How she found me is still a mystery or a miracle, depending on your perspective. Any way you slice it, I'm lucky she was there, though showing gratitude for it wouldn't come easy for a long time after. How she put up with me for as long as she did is pure miracle, no mystery about it. She's as close to an angel as I'll ever get. Whenever I think of her, I always remember the way she looked there by the river; long auburn hair, glistening hazel eyes and a T-shirt that read *Zombies Hate Fast Food.*

When she reached out and took my hand, it shattered my world. Her eyes and the warm press of her skin against mine changed everything. Suddenly I was gasping for breath, fighting for life, and as she lowered her face to within inches of mine, I felt my heart slam painfully in my chest. She parted her lips, making me believe she would kiss me goodbye. If that had been the last sensation I experienced in this world I would have died a lucky man. Instead, she whispered one word against my mouth. One word that would press air into my lungs and pull me back from the void.

"Breathe."

Then she was gone.

Chapter One

Alex

I wake with a start. My eyes immediately find the black sparrow decals flying across the white paint of the wall beside my bed, calming my racing heart. I trace one with my fingers, smiling at the familiar feel of its edges. This is what I always do. This is how they tell me that I'm home.

I actually hate birds. They're too quick and erratic with their sharp claws and beaks. They're like flying, disease carrying knives. But more than anything I hate them because they remind me of the Dragon.

"Are you here?" Cara calls.

"Present and accounted for." I drop my hand from the bird just as my bedroom door swings open. My sister stands in the doorway. Watching.

"You okay?"

"Yeah, I'm good."

"I'm glad you're home."

I chuckle quietly. It could go without saying but she says it every time. "Me too."

"Where'd you go? Do I want to know?"

"Transylvania." I lie.

"Okay, so I don't want to know."

I shake my head. No. She doesn't want to know.

"I had the Dragon Dream." I tell her, changing the subject. "It brought me home."

"The Jabberwocky." she corrects me quickly.

I roll my eyes. "It's not the Jabberwocky."

"I have shown you the pictures. It looks exactly as you described."

"I know, but—"

"Is it or is it not the spitting image of the Jabberwocky?"

"It is." I concede, before quickly adding, "But how would I have started dreaming of the Jabberwocky when I was four years old? We never had the book."

"You saw the movie."

"We've talked about this." I groan. "The Disney *Alice* doesn't have the Jabberwocky in it. There's no way. It's not him, it's just a dragon."

"It'd be cool if you could dream about *Pete's Dragon*."

"Jesus, don't put the idea in my head!"

"What? He's friendly! And it's not like you can Slip to Passamaquody."

Slip is our word for what I do. For my tendency to fall asleep, dream of New York City and wake up in Times Square in my underwear. My parents called it sleep walking though it's not at all accurate. It just made it sound normal, made it easier for them. I don't stand up and walk out the door. When I Slip, I dream of a place then there I am. The base of the Eiffel Tower. The shore on the coast of Ireland. The third baseline at Wrigley Field. While it can take my mind a millisecond to raise familiar images of the Las Vegas strip, it will take me days to return my body home from it. I don't understand how it happens. No one does. It's mind over matter to the nth degree. It is unpredictable, terrifying, and most of all, annoying.

"He kicked my ass." I tell her glumly, thinking of the Dragon. I rub my leg even though there's no wound on it. Not anymore. Not now that I'm awake.

"Jabberwocky's are the worst."

"It's not the Jabberwocky!"

"Sure. Hey, what are we doing tonight? Did you decide?"

I throw my arm across my face. "Nothing, we are doing nothing."

"No," she insists, pulling my arm away. "We were going to do nothing if you Slipped away to Antarctica. But you didn't. You're here and we need to celebrate."

"It's not a big one. Can't we just let it slide?"

"Every birthday until your twenty-second is a big one. Your twenty-second is a bust. From there on out you receive no new liberties, other than the right to grow old."

"That's depressing."

"It is, so enjoy the good ones while you can. You're turning twenty! This is a big deal." She takes my hand in hers and squeezes it affectionately. "Plus, you got shafted pretty hard on your last few birthdays. They should have been special and I know they really weren't. Let's use this year to make up for it."

For my Sweet Sixteen my parents gave me an eviction notice and a new car. Worst Showcase Showdown ever. Since then birthdays have held little appeal to me seeing as I now associate them with abandonment and hush money.

My sister is eight years older than I am and was already an established, responsible adult when I got the boot. She's a Certified Public Accountant making good money and was more than happy to take me in. She knew what was wrong with me, knew she'd have to support me because I can't hold down a job, but she didn't care. When I showed up at her door, a lost, crying mess, she promised that she'd always watch out for me. Then she went to our parent's house, took my things, gave them a piece of her mind and never looked back. She's fiercely protective of me and I want to say it bothers me and that I can take care of myself, but after growing up with a mother who kept me at a distance, knowing someone has my back is indescribable.

"Can we egg their house?" I ask, referring to our parents.

"No. But I will buy a big ass Margarita and let you take hits off it."

"Deal."

∞

I'm standing on the bank of the Missouri River in Omaha, wondering why I work so hard to stay here. I should embrace the escape and let my mind Slip me far, far away to a place that is warm. My hands are freezing and my toes would ache if they could remember what it was like to feel.

Cara brought me here to try and use her old driver's license to get me into the casinos, but I'm having doubts. Doubts I like to call Mango Margarita: The Devil's Drink. Or El Bebir Del Diablo? I don't know, I didn't do well in high school Spanish. I Slipped to Mexico once and it was a complete disaster. Turns out *hambre* and *hombre* are easily confused and when you adamantly insist in broken Spanglish that you be in possession of one, it doesn't always get you a burrito. Sometimes it gets you a male prostitute. Who knew brothels had a lunch menu?

Cara is up at the car waiting for her work friends to join us while I and my dubious stomach have taken a walk to the river in case of emergency. I'm not fond of the idea of barfing in the parking lot in plain view of everyone. At the moment, I am not fond of anything.

I'm surveying the frozen beach, looking for somewhere to sit and wait out my troubles, when I spot the body. It's a man, ghostly white and lying in the shallow waters of the freezing river. Before my brain knows what's happening, I'm rushing down the shore, tripping over mounds of snow and ice slicked rocks until I collapse on my knees beside him.

He looks to be about my age, his pale skin contrasting sharply with his buzzed black hair. He's naked except for a black Speedo-esque swimsuit. Even to my drunk mind, that seems like weird attire for December in Nebraska. I quickly strip off my heavy coat and throw it over his chest, shivering immediately in just my T-shirt. I don't see his chest rising or falling so I grab for his hand to take his pulse. Relief floods through me when I find his skin is relatively warm and pliant. I'm hoping this means he's not dead yet.

The second I touch him, he lurches forward as though I shocked him. His arms and legs spasm wildly before he leans over to cough. He ends up puking almost directly into my lap. It's all liquid but I smell something chemical in it, something vaguely familiar. I wonder if it's some kind of alcohol. He drops back down hard onto the rocks, but they don't make a sound with the impact. I watch as he stares unblinking at the sky, lying so still I think he must be dead now. I may have just witnessed death throws.

I rub his hand between both of mine and lean close,

so close our noses are almost touching and my hair falls around us. His eyes latch onto mine and I gasp at how bright they are. How brilliantly green. How utterly alive. I whisper one word to him, the only thing I can think to say.

"Breathe."

He vanishes. My coat is lying on wet stones, my hand is holding cold air.

My heart stops beating. My breath freezes in my lungs. I clench my hands tightly, feeling them tingle and itch where my skin met his. He was real. I held his hand and I'm awake. I know that I'm awake. There's no way that was a dream.

"What the hell?" I whisper, my voice quivering.

This is it. This is insanity taking hold. I'm breaking from reality. I'm losing my mind, though it never fully felt like mine to begin with.

Trembling from the cold, shock and a growing fear, I grab my jacket to pull it on. I can't get my hands to work right. The zipper feels painfully cold between my fingertips and I abandon any hope of closing it. Standing quickly, I run back across the rocks and up the bank to my sister's car. By the time I get there I'm nearly hyperventilating.

Her friends have arrived and they're standing in a halo of streetlight, clouds of warm breath rising around them in the cold air. Cara sees me and my anxiety must be on my face because she rushes over.

"What's wrong? Were you sick?" she asks, touching my arm. She frowns and pulls her hand back. "Your coat is wet."

"Yeah."

"Did you puke on your coat?" she asks, her face disgusted.

I think of the guy leaning over and throwing up river water.

"Yeah." I mumble.

"Gross. I think you're done for the night."

"Me too." I say eagerly. I nod but it's more of a convulsion and I practically run for the car.

Cara says a hasty goodbye to her friends who laugh in understanding. Once inside, she cranks the heat and eyes me, watching me shake.

"You sure you're okay?"

"I just want to go to sleep."

"That's a first." she says, but leaves it at that.

Over the years Cara has learned that I don't like to talk about half the stuff that goes on when I'm asleep. I've seen things and been places that I don't like to revisit, waking or otherwise.

"What's that smell?" she asks suddenly.

"My dinner's second coming."

"No, you smell like a swimming pool." She scrunches up her nose and glances sideways at me. "Like chlorine."

This night is getting weirder by the second. I vow to never drink again.

About the Author

I was born in Eugene, Oregon and studied English Literature at the University of Oregon (Go Ducks!) It was there that I discovered why Latin is a dead language and that being an English teacher was not actually what I wanted to do with my life.

My husband, my son and my 80lbs pitbull who thinks he's a lapdog are my world.

Visit my website for more information on upcoming releases, www.traceywardauthor.com

Made in the USA
San Bernardino, CA
01 November 2014